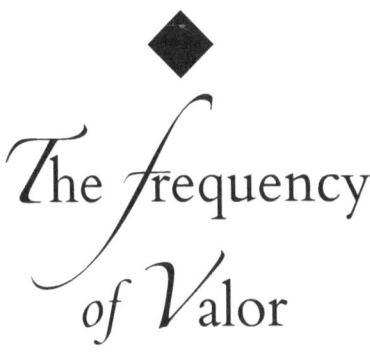

The Frequency of Valor

A NOVELLA

A Tale of Romance & Intrigue Inspired by True Events that Occurred During WWII at a Spy Station in Rhode Island and a Luxurious Paris Hotel

Jan French

DEDICATED TO

Ruth & Kenneth French

An Aeroplane Series Book

I. The Mysterious Man

He drives slowly down the long, wooded road. He is dressed smartly, wearing a grey felt hat embellished with a black silk band. His grey pin-striped suit is slightly wrinkled, his white shirt is crisp with a stiffly pressed collar. The sun is beginning its slow descent to the west, allowing the trees to cast shadows across the dirt road. Storm clouds have formed in the sky, mirroring the dark climate of the times. 'I'll Never Smile Again' by Tommy Dorsey plays on his radio. He smiles at the irony of the song.

He is tired yet he is determined to drive on. The tires on his 1939 black Ford Coupe kick up a dust cloud behind him.

A little girl with unkempt golden locks is gathering daisies along the dusty dirt road and is placing them in a red rusted pail. She stops in her tracks and stares as the man drives by. She smiles and gives this curious person a big wave, squinting against the setting sun. She breaks into a run to chase the mysterious shiny black car driving so briskly on a road that is more frequented by work horses, tractors and crossing cattle. She loses ground and slows to a jog, bending over to catch her breath. She backtracks to collect the daisies that have escaped her little pail.

A farmer smudged with the dirt of a long day stops feeding his horse to watch the car pass by, hay falls silently from his calloused hand to settle on the ground below him. His expression holds a mixture of curiosity and dismay.

It is clear that neither one of them has ever seen a car so grand make its way down their road. The smart looking man from Boston drives on. He is the bearer of unsettling news.

II.   The Suddard Farm

He is driving to the Suddard Farm, located in a remote part of Rhode Island in a town called Scituate. The farm is located on the top of a peak called Chopmist Hill. His name is Thomas Cave and he works for RID (Radio Intelligence Division), a subdivision of the FCC (Federal Communications Commission).

It is April 2nd, 1941, months before the United States is destined to enter WWII. Cave and others working in the intelligence sector maintain that it is just a matter of time before the United States is pulled into the war that has been raging in Europe. His task is to find an ideal location for a spy monitoring station in southern New England. It is time for the U.S. to begin rooting out domestic and foreign spies working against the allies. It is time to locate any clandestine radio stations operating on American soil and beyond. This can only be done by listening in.

Cave has found the perfect site at the Suddard Farm, located at the top of Chopmist Hill. He has discovered that the Chopmist Hill location has the uncanny ability to pick up signals from far away, outmatching all other tested sites.

It is also Cave's job to break the news to the Suddard family that they must leave their beloved farm for the

good of the cause……and no; they do not have a choice.
They must vacate their farm so that RID (Radio Intelligence Division) can set up post and transform this beautiful old farmhouse and fields into a spy listening station.
It is time to replace the trees, crops and old wooden barns
that have existed on this farm for over one hundred years
with steel.

Thomas Cave slows his car to a stop on the gravel
driveway next to the old Victorian farmhouse. As he sits
there gathering his thoughts he sees Mr. Suddard behind
an old screen door, he is wearing brown corduroy pants
and an old plaid shirt which has been lovingly worn at the
elbows. He opens the door to stand on his porch. Cave
can see, even at a distance, the sadness in his eyes. He is a
kind man, a gentle man, a man who has tended this farm
his entire life. He is sixty-eight years old, too young to
leave his family farm, too old to fight for it.

Cave can tell by the slump of his shoulders that Mr.
Suddard has already figured out why he has returned to
his farm. Of course he does, the FCC wouldn't be sending Cave to tell him they had found a better location, a
location that was not his beloved farm. They would have
said nothing at all; they would have left him wondering if
they would ever return.

Quite the opposite though, the location is perfect. The
radio transmissions are the best Cave has discovered in
his exhausting travels. Months before, he visited several
possible sites in Southern New England. He found some
were acceptable. But his visit to Chopmist Hill gave him
exactly what he was looking for, transmissions that were

clearer and more far-reaching than any he had previously found.

When he first stumbled upon this site he was truly amazed. He attributed the extraordinary reception to the height of Chopmist Hill. It is approximately six hundred feet above sea level, eliminating any other technical interference for many miles. The remoteness of the farm ensured that the radio transmissions would be clear of any other radio activity nearby therefore eliminating any interruptions. But Cave will not realize the full potential until all the state-of-the-art equipment is put into place.

Cave hesitates before opening his car door. He has been rehearsing exactly what he needs to say. He needs to be direct yet show compassion. It is a difficult combination.

As he gets out of his car, just a nod will do. In spite of Cave's sudden appearance, William Suddard offers a warm smile which speaks of grace and kindness from another time.

He motions Cave to come in. They sit at an old farm table in the kitchen. The table is scratched, worn and dented. William pours him a freshly made cup of coffee. Cave takes his black. As he sips his coffee he glances down into the chipped mug he is handed, delaying the inevitable eye contact with William. His eye strays to the tabletop. He smiles as he sees a childlike carving in the wood. '*Theo was here*'. He envisions the family packing up all the old worn dishes, clothes, furniture, and memories forever stilled in photographs.

"I imagine you have already figured out why I am here. Out of all the locations I have visited in Southern

New England, this farm of yours is just what we are looking for. Without going into much detail, the government
of the United States would like to lease your property
indefinitely. For reasons of security, I cannot disclose
what your property will be used for. It would be temporary, until the war in Europe is over." Thomas explains.

"I had a feeling you'd be back. The last time you were
here, you stayed for quite a while. You seemed fascinated
by the old place. You know, my family has farmed on this
property for one hundred and fifty years. How long do
you think you'll have to stay here? How long until we can
return? Can I simply say no we're not leaving?" William
asks Thomas.

"Unfortunately, you cannot say no. And I cannot
give you a date of when you can return either." Thomas
replies honestly. "Some say this war won't last long. But
from what I can tell the Germans have built up quite an
impressive army. I believe it's only a matter of time before
we are pulled into it and it's going to be an uphill battle
for our side. It will probably be sooner rather than later
that we get involved. From what I can see, it looks like
Hitler is bent on conquering the entire world and he's in
a hurry to do it." He adds.

"Well, my wife and I have relatives we can stay with
until this war plays itself out. Don't worry about us. They
say change can do you good." William assures Thomas.
William can see that Thomas is clearly struggling with
this awkward encounter.

"I know this is a tough situation Mr. Suddard. A real
inconvenience for you and your wife and I'm sorry about

that. We truly appreciate your cooperation regarding this. Hopefully, this war will play itself out quickly and you can return home to your farm soon." Thomas says trying to console William in some way.

A feeling of uncertainty and apprehension settles in Thomas's heart. He realizes that their future has been interrupted and forever changed by his decision alone. He discovered the location, and he made the final decision to locate the listening post here at this farm. He tries to push the feeling aside, convincing himself that this is the right thing to do. But just enough doubt lingers to give guilt a home. Cave is aware that there is no guarantee that the Suddard's will ever step foot on their farm again. Wartime selfishly holds captive any glimpse of a light at the end of a long dark tunnel.

He tries to imagine what it must feel like to leave a farm so devotedly tended to for so many generations. Paintings and old photographs will be removed from the plastered walls, revealing the brighter un-faded paint that still exists behind them. They leave a poignant reminder of how long the Suddard's have lived and loved in this old farmhouse.

They obligingly agree to lease their property to the FCC and leave; they realized it is for the good of their country and the allies and that they really don't have any other choice anyway.

III. The Departure

Thomas informs William he has a month to move his family and belongings out of the farmhouse. During this time, the RID will be setting up house.

The treeless farm fields will soon be home to telephone poles, barracks, and a radio tower made of steel. Miles of wires will be brought in, wired to listen to voices far away. Thirty men and women will be stationed at the farm as the 'listeners'.

Their task is to locate clandestine radio stations and equipment being used illegally. They are also recruited to intercept all of the radio transmissions that are being transmitted by any known enemy. These intercepted messages will then be sent on to the Pentagon to be decoded, interpreted, and analyzed. Only then can action be taken by the U.S. or its allies.

William stands at the kitchen window looking out on his farm. The construction has already begun. There are jeeps of dull green dotting the farmland, men yelling orders here and there. Where cornfields once stood with crops reaching for the sun, bulldozers dig and level the soil. William Suddard bears witness to the rapid disappearance of his farm.

Construction of the out-buildings has begun, changing

the landscape into an unrecognizable place. A place that has been untouched for so many years is suddenly catching up with the times. The farm is entering the twentieth century of war technology and change. It is entering a time when simplicity is cast aside for complexity. The quiet pasture and acres of vegetable plantings will be leveled. Nothing will remain the same; the landscape will be forever altered.

William's wife Laura sits behind him at the kitchen table packing her wedding china; she carefully wraps it in the newspapers they have saved. It is Royal Doulton Bone China, one of the only luxuries they possess. The beautiful pattern of the china is in contrast with the black and white news-printed paper she wraps it in. She was coaxed by her mother to register at Tilden Thurber & Co. in Providence prior to her wedding in the Spring of 1912. She believes no one will buy it because it is far too expensive. But they do. She has six plates, a creamer and sugar bowl, four teacups with saucers and a teapot. It is the violet pattern, her favorite flower.

William turns from the window to look at his wife. She is wearing a floral dress of yellow roses, his favorite dress. A birthday gift he bought for her many years ago. At that moment, he could not love her more. She is humming a song, as if it is just another ordinary day…. '*Somewhere over the Rainbow.*'

He knows she does this for him, and his sadness is replaced with thoughts of her bravery. Thoughts of her innocent way of protecting him from the misery that has taken hold of his heart.

"Everything will be fine, you'll see." he says to her not

believing a word he says. "I know, I know." She replies, not
believing a word either. She continues wrapping the china
slowly as if it will somehow delay the impending move;
their silence fills the room until they can hardly breath.

As Laura continues to wrap her china, she thinks back
to her wedding day so long ago. It was a May wedding,
warm and breezy. They married here at the farm, a tradition dating back one hundred years. Every Suddard
wedding has taken place at this farm. She smiles as she
remembers William's proposal.

"If you want to marry me, you will have to marry me
at the farm. It's a tradition and we will be forever cursed if
we don't." he says as he grabs her tiny waist and easily lifts
her off her bare feet to hold her above him. She holds on
to his shoulders to keep herself suspended there for as long
as possible so she can look down into his handsome face.
He has proposed to her under an ancient tree in a field
close to the farm. It will become their favorite picnic spot
in the years to come. He slowly brings her down until her
toes touch the ground and now she is looking up at him.

"Yes, I will marry you William Suddard……and I will
marry you on your dusty old farm." She answers as they
both laugh.

She remembers the first time William brought her
to the farm. She fell in love with it straightaway. Her
first glimpse was the expansive stonewall enclosing the
entire farm. Then the cobble stone walkway leading to
the house, each side endowed with a row of French lavender. The house, built in 1870, replacing the original
cape that was built in 1785. It is a mixture of Victorian

and farmhouse. Elegant and practicable at the same time. A wide and comfortable front porch on the first floor is topped with two Victorian peaks. The second floor holds the details of gingerbread trim tucked into the points. It is a beautiful old gem that needs the gentle touch of a woman. Over the years Laura will transform the house back to its original glory. A labor of love, although she only remembers the love now.

William places his hand on her shoulder, and it brings her back to the present. She looks around and realizes that the packing is complete. She feels as if she has packed up her memories as well. Years and years of memories. Perhaps she will leave some of the boxes unopened after they move away. Best to keep old memories safely stowed away, else they bring to mind unbidden longings.

William and Laura fall exhausted onto their old wrought iron bed, which has been repainted a dozen times. The old mattress springs creak under their weight. They both reach at the same time and pull crisp white sheets fresh from the clothesline to cover them. This is followed by a hand-sewn quilt, a wedding gift from his mother. It is made up of pieces of fabric dating back at least one hundred years. Scrapes saved up for quilting, stored in an old cedar chest.

They roll to face each other. The moonlight has softened the lines on their faces giving them back some of their youth. Laura thinks of their wedding night, so long ago. It was exactly the same. Except when they rolled to face each other all those years ago, they were giddy with laughter and anticipation.

Now they have a different kind of restless night ahead of them. They kiss and drift off to sleep still facing each other. Their grey tiger-striped cat settles in his familiar spot, the nook made by her bended knees.

They both dream of the house they are leaving; it holds them captive for one more night. A love letter. A final goodbye.

Laura dreams of William coming through the screen door in the back of the house, it slaps but never quite closes. Since they have lived there, it has never found the latch properly. He repeatedly says, "I need to fix that". But he never does. She is at the stove stirring soup in an old, dented pan. He comes up behind her and wraps his arms around her tiny waist. She leans into him; the scent of the old barn rises from his flannel shirt, a mixture of hay, earth, and sweat.

William dreams he is running into the kitchen to get out of the rain. He sees Laura's slender back, beautiful, and strong standing over the kitchen sink. She is rinsing vegetables in her mother's old blue enamel colander, and he can't wait to reach her and bury his head in her hair. She smells of lavender and ivory soap. She bends her head to one side as he kisses her neck. The room fills with their love and their laughter.

They both awake with a start at the same time. They stare at the old, cracked bedroom ceiling for the very last time. The old crystal chandelier, original to the house and fashioned just for candles, sways slightly with a silent wave goodbye.

Although the Suddard's are hopeful they will return to

their farm one day when the war is over, they never do. The government will hold on to their farm for a full ten years. Sadly, too many changes in their lives will prevent a homecoming.

The Suddard's leave one day earlier than the month they are given. As they drive away, they cannot look back. They keep their sadness buried deep, buried in the land they leave behind. Laura absentmindedly strokes the cat as it sits contentedly on her lap. They pass the old tree where William proposed to her, it has fallen. Its aging roots have been uplifted by a strong stormy wind. It begins its journey of slow decay, making its way back into the earth it came from.

The old pick-up truck kicks up the same dust on the way out that Thomas Cave kicked up on his way in..... 29 days ago.

IV.   The Transformation

Thomas is busy overseeing the entire operation. The fourteen-room farmhouse is totally transformed. Six of the downstairs rooms are loaded with the latest equipment including highly sensitive radio receivers and transmitters.

The farmland, which consists of one hundred and forty acres, is equipped with telephone poles, miles and miles of wire, a massive radio tower reaching far beyond the treetops.

Barracks are built for the thirty 'listeners' coming in from all over the country. Outbuildings are built to house additional radio equipment. The farmland that once held fields for crops is hardly recognizable anymore. The exterior of the farmhouse is the only thing left intact, in sharp contrast to the industrial components and buildings that now surround it.

All surrounding neighbors are kept in the dark regarding the purpose of the listening station. Rumors swirl, but no one knows for sure what is going on at the Suddard farm. Even the thirty listeners recruited to work at the station for RID are not yet fully aware of the significance or magnitude of what they are about to get involved in.

The transformation is just about complete. Thomas is satisfied that they will be able to intercept domestic spies operating within the United States, the initial purpose of the station. The station location is highly sensitive and seems to be able to pick up a wide array of signals from various radio transmitters. The task now is to weed out the clandestine stations operated by the enemy.

V. The Listeners

There are Twenty-six men and four women employed as radio operating personnel at Chopmist Hill. Most have amateur radio operating skills. Some are brought in because of their technical and engineering skills while others are brought in for their command of foreign languages including German, French and Italian.

There are two Quonset hut barracks made of prefabricated steel assembled to house the men. The four women are given two rooms and a shared bathroom upstairs in the old farmhouse. They work in shifts, as the listening must be carried out twenty-four hours a day, seven days a week. The work is taxing. Every unregistered and clandestine station being discovered must be recorded and filed. This includes the time of day they are typically active, so they can be monitored on a regular basis. They cannot afford to miss anything that could go unchecked because of inattention to detail.

Their down time is spent sleeping, playing cards, reading, listening to news and music on the radio and an occasional trip to the city of Providence and other Rhode Island destinations for a quick supper or dancing.

Most meals are taken in the farmhouse kitchen in shifts of ten. The men and women are all regarded as equals, something quite unique for the time. They all pitch in on the chores, including meals and clean up.

They are allowed one weekend a month to travel home or elsewhere if they desire. Quite frequently the ones who are married travel home. The ones that are single don't go home as often and begin to spend more and more time traveling to Providence and surrounding areas to visit the popular nightclubs and restaurants.

The Biltmore Hotel and Rhodes-on-the-Pawtuxet become their favorite haunts because they both have ballrooms that bring in the most talented 'big bands' in the Northeast and beyond. The visits to Providence provide a much-needed escape from the grueling and challenging work they are assigned to.

VI. The Ultimate Test

Thomas is sitting at his post one morning just days after settling in at the station. He zeroes in on a signal from a transmitter coming from what seems to be somewhere in either Washington D.C. or close by in Virginia.

"What do we have here?" He says out loud without realizing it.

Jaime, one of the newly recruited listeners, overhears him.

"What's up?" Jaime asks.

"Odd, I'm picking up an unregistered clandestine signal, coming from Washington D.C., close to the Pentagon perhaps?" Thomas replies. "Spies at the Pentagon?" Jaime asks. "Better get this straight over to the Chief" Thomas says, referring to the Chief of the FCC.

Thomas makes a call to alert The Chief immediately.

"Well, well, well, Thomas. I had the army set up a fake test. They sent out phony signals. Truthfully, we didn't think they would be picked up so quickly if picked up at all. Your post is the first to respond! Remarkable, absolutely remarkable!" says The Chief.

"Congratulations Thomas Cave. Your Chopmist Hill station has won! It took you seven minutes! Unheard of! Completely, unheard of! Well done!" exclaims The Chief.

Thomas gathers all the listeners and informs them of the good news. The room erupts in applause and cheers.

"Ok you bunch of crazy spies! Get back to work! We have some Nazi's to hunt down!" he says, which is met with laughter and more cheers.

VII.   The Business of Spying

Thomas Cave settles in and gets down to the business of tuning in and locating clandestine radio stations being used by enemy spies. With all the equipment finally in place, he will be able to determine the stations full potential. As he tunes into the frequencies the listening post is able to locate, he leans back and exhales all of the breath left in his lungs.

"Oh, for heaven's sake, this cannot be possible." he says in disbelief. He is picking up someone speaking in the German language. He quickly changes frequencies to the next channel….and the next…..and the next. As he continues, the gravity of the listening station's potential leaves him stunned and speechless. He is intercepting messages from Germany.

"Good god! Can this really be happening?" he says to himself.

He is so transfixed; it takes him a long while before he can gain his composure and start to listen again. He needs to be sure that he is correct in his assumption. He needs to be sure he has not lost control of his senses.

Thomas settles back into his chair and tunes back in. He calls over Jaime, the only Rhode Islander in the group. Jaime is only twenty-one years old. He was recruited after answering the ad in the Providence Journal to come and work for Uncle Sam.

He is the son of German immigrants who fled Berlin toward the end of WWI after seeing a rise in anti-Semitism. Jaime's mother is Jewish, so his parents decide to move to America because she is pregnant and fears that her child will also be exposed to the racism that is gaining momentum in Germany.

Because his parents speak mostly German at home, Jaime is fluent in German and has a Berlin accent. This and Jaime's exceptional engineering skills are the main reasons he has been recruited as a Chopmist Hill 'listener'. Jaime displays such exceptional skills; The FCC is keeping an eye on him for quick advancement. There is also the possibility of sending him on assignments that will require someone who speaks fluent German.

He is an attractive young man, tall and thin. Yet his wide shoulders tell of a confident young man. He has intense hazel eyes. He sports the latest and most fashionable suit. He is handsome in a way that shows the transformation from a boy to a man. Thomas can surmise he is an intelligent, bright and eager young man.

"Take a listen, will you Jaime. What do you make of it?" Thomas asks.

"Well sir, it's definitely the German language coming straight out of Berlin as far as I can tell. Yes indeed, no doubt about it. I'll be.....I'll be a son of a gun Sir!!!! It can't be! Can it be Mr. Cave? Are we picking up transmissions from Europe?....from Germany?" asks Jaime.

"It looks that way Jaime! Incredible as it seems! At

first I thought it could be coming from somewhere in the States, but the frequency is coming from abroad." Thomas replies.

Thomas lets him listen to more and more frequencies. They both sit in silence for what seems an eternity. The others in the room feel the silent energy and they all start to gather around the two stunned men. They wait in quiet anticipation for an explanation.

As they continue the listening in the days to come, they discover the listening post is so far-reaching they are able to pick up faint static transmissions all the way from Australia.

What Thomas Cave discovers is the impossible. It is nothing short of a miracle. This sloping hill that Thomas has discovered in his search for the right location has the uncanny ability to reach every continent on the globe. It has the ability to pick up the weakest of signals from the most treacherous of enemies. They will be able to listen in on approximately four hundred enemy transmitting posts, including a clandestine station set up by the Germans in West Africa to spy on British shipping activity.

They will also discover that South America has an abundant number of clandestine stations operated by the Germans. All are located and shut down with the exception of any located in Argentina, a country that has sided with the enemy.

The enemies of the allies will eventually meet their demise thanks in part to a small spy station monitored by thirty men and women stationed on a hill. A beautiful sloping hill in the small country town of Scituate, RI, called Chopmist Hill.

VIII. Infamy

It is late November of 1941; Gia Franzese is sitting at her station at the post. She is intently listening in. Thomas notices that whenever Gia intercepts something important or perplexing she starts to twirl her short hair with her fingers and a deep line of worry forms between her brows.

Gia is an exceptionally intelligent and dedicated girl. Thomas feels fortunate that she was recruited for this listening post. Born in Brooklyn, she is the daughter of Italian immigrants. Landing on Ellis Island in 1915, they will settle in the Bensonhurst neighborhood of Brooklyn, New York.

Her parents, Anthony and Angela promptly opened a small corner bakery that will carry baked breads and Italian pastries. The recipe's all come from Italy, passed down from generation to generation.

Gia and her brother Joey help out in the kitchen, growing up covered in flour. They always wait by the oven for the cookies to come out, their mother always passing them each their favorite treat. Gia will always reach for Struffoli, cookies dredged in honey. Joey will always reach for Sfogliatelle, pastry filled with ricotta.

Gia's parents do well throughout the depression, managing to keep the Bakery operating despite a failing economy. However, they do not have the means to send Gia to art school to become a graphic designer, her dream. So, she applies for the civil servant job working at a monitoring station, among many other qualified applicants, not thinking she has a chance. However, she passes the test with high grades and is hired immediately. She makes a promise to herself she will pursue her dream and go to art school after the war in Europe is over and she has saved enough money to afford the tuition.

Thomas strides over and gently pulls one side of her earphones away from her ear.

"What is it Gia? I can tell by your expression that you have tuned into something pretty significant." he says.

"Um, is anyone else picking up activity in the Pacific?" she asks. "I'm picking up signals from the waters close to Japan. Coded….lots of activity" she informs Thomas.

She rolls back in her chair and crashes into the back of Jaime's chair. This is a daily occurrence, since they are in such a cramped space. Jaime doesn't mind this frequent mishap; in fact he looks forward to it. Most times they laugh and roll back to their limited space. Sometimes Jaime manages to start up a conversation. To his delight, the conversations have gotten longer and longer.

But today is different, strictly business. It is clear something ominous is on the horizon. The air is thick with anticipation. Something is amiss.

"Jesus." replies Thomas in an astonished whisper. He quickly alerts the others to tune in.

"Over here" shouts Tommy Miller. Others chime in. It seems the Pacific waters near Japan have become quite crowded with an abundance of coded transmissions.

Thomas Cave and his team of listeners start to intercept numerous messages of Japanese movements in the Pacific and pass on these messages to Washington prior to the attack on December 7th., 1941.

It is clear to Cave that some sort of an attack is imminent. Unfortunately, not enough information connects the intercepted messages to the Pearl Harbor location.

To the shock and horror of the entire country, the imminent attack takes place. The day following the attack on Pearl Harbor, the United States declares war on Japan.

It is a somber day at the monitoring station at Chopmist Hill. They all wonder if they missed something, perhaps a message that would have provided the exact location of the attack on Pearl Harbor.

Thomas is aware of the dark mood that has taken hold of the station, so he gathers everyone together.

"Look, I know how all of you are feeling right now. I feel the same way. The whole country does. It's devastating, absolutely devastating. But I have been right here with all of you, all along. Believe me when I tell you, you did everything right. All of you did. We cannot go back; we can only go forward and carry on. All I can say is…... We are in it now! Now let's get back to work and win this bloody war!" Thomas says with resolve.

Three days after the Pearl Harbor attack, the Germans and Italians declare war on the U.S.

The inevitable day has arrived. The United States is at war. Now more than ever, the importance of the Chopmist Hill monitoring station is crucial to the war effort. It is imperative in the effort to collect enemy strategy and follow enemy movements on both fronts.

IX.   The Miraculous Interception

It is early in the year of 1942 and Jason Burford is stationed at his post within the farmhouse when he hears the German language being spoken. Not familiar with the language, he calls on Jaime to take a listen.

"Definitely speaking German, Tough to say what is being said" says Jaime. Thomas overhears Jason and Jaime's conversation and strides over to listen in.

"What's going on? What are you hearing?" Thomas asks.

"Sort of sounds like commands possibly coming from a battlefield? German language. Sounds like tank movements. Can't be possible. The signal is coming from North Africa?" Jaime says in disbelief.

"Jesus! That's impossible. We can't possibly be picking up signals from tanks in North Africa! German tanks? We can't have that kind of reception!" says Cave.

But he is wondering if perhaps they do have that kind of reception. After all, the reception at Chopmist Hill is extraordinary, like nothing he has ever encountered before. There is no doubt about that in Cave's mind, given what has transpired at the station.

Cave is aware that German General Erwin Rommel is in North Africa. This would be an unbelievable coup if they are listening in on commands coming straight from Rommel or his commanders and soldiers. He is pushing ahead and winning the battles in North Africa against the British. If they are truly intercepting tank-to-tank messages between Rommel and his troops, this would be a game changer.

"Get this transcribed and on to Washington NOW!" Cave yells.

They wait in earnest for feedback on the incredible interception. Finally, Cave hears back from the staff at the FCC. The Pentagon has confirmed it is tank-to-tank transmissions. They have done the impossible at Chopmist Hill. They have intercepted tank-to-tank messages between Rommel and his troops.

"Jaime, get on it! These are messages between Rommel and his troops! This is your task from now on!" Cave says to Jaime.

From this day forward they are able to determine Rommel's strategy and movements in North Africa. Being alerted in advance by intelligence retrieved at Chopmist Hill, British General Bernard Montgomery and his troops will be ready to battle it out with Rommel and they will succeed. This information will eventually contribute to the victory of the Battle of El Alamein in Egypt by the allies, forever eliminating the hold Rommel has had on North Africa. It is a decisive turning point in the war.

X.   The Providence Biltmore

Jason leans back on his chair and stretches. It has been quite a day. He has the night off and contemplates heading into Providence for a drink or heading to bed.

"Anyone wanna head to the Biltmore?" Jason asks. "I'm up for it." replies Tommy Miller. "Me too!" replies Jaime. "Take me too!" Gia chimes in.

Jaime turns in his chair to gaze at Gia. She is busy typing, transcribing recorded tapes. Her back is facing him, and he glances at her long, graceful neck and he smiles. He is pleased she is joining them on their night out at the Biltmore.

When he first saw her entering the farmhouse, struggling with her suitcase, he had to catch his breath before he jumped up to help her carry in her belongings. She is quite different from anyone he has ever met in the small town of Chepachet RI, where he grew up. Her hairstyle is pixie short and bleach blonde. She wears trousers and a crisp white button-down shirt during the day. She is tall and slender with wide shoulders that compliment her strong personality. Her demeanor is blunt and to the point. She is not a glamor girl, but she is attractive in a smart sort of way. Jaime gathers she must have been a tomboy growing up.

More importantly, she laughs at his silly jokes, without

reservation. Her laugh is naturally loud and raspy. She is a New Yorker. She is smart and silly, warm and cool, cautious and daring. A complex and interesting mix, Jaime surmises.

They all retreat to change into their evening clothes. Gia returns wearing a pencil straight black skirt and an ivory angora sweater tucked in, it accentuates her small waist. White gloves, high-heeled tan swede pumps and a black silk purse. Red lipstick. He can see that she has attempted to draw a black line up the back of her legs to simulate the stockings that have been rationed off her beautiful long legs. She has missed a section just above her left ankle, Jaime realizes that his eyes are traveling the length of her legs and he quickly looks away.

The rationing makes Jaime think of his Mum. Being a Rhode Islander, he is fortunate to have her nearby. He visits her every other Tuesday, his day off. She informs him that they have rationed real butter right out of her pie making hands and she is using margarine, fake butter she calls it. But to Jaime, her pies still taste delicious. She always makes two extras for Jaime to bring back to the monitoring post. Strawberry Rhubarb and Blueberry have become the favorites of the listeners.

He worries for his parents. Being German, they have had their share of hostilities coming from some of their neighbors. Americans have become very suspicious of anyone of German descent, especially immigrants born in Germany. Jaime hopes it will pass as soon as the war ends. Everyone is over confidant that the war won't last too long. Jaime has his doubts.

Jamie is quite taken with Gia. He remembers something his father said to him long ago about the first time he saw Jaime's mother.

"From the moment I saw her, all the others were forgotten. She became my past, my present and my future all in one second." Jaime now understands what his father was trying to convey. His father was describing love at first sight, something Jaime never used to believe in. He is now happily rethinking many of his old theories regarding love, because of the way he felt the moment he saw Gia. The rest of his surroundings became a blur. All the other voices and sounds in the room went mute. It was as if time had stopped. She was standing there framed by the doorway of the old farmhouse, it doubled as a picture frame to hold an extraordinary work of art.

Jaime is at a loss for words and struggles to join in on the conversation during the drive to Providence. He has suddenly become shy and self-conscience in front of mixed company. The other two men take over the conversation as Jaime sits in the back seat thinking of something interesting to say. He gives up and hopes Gia thinks he's the strong silent type. He smirks at this thought and is glad it is too dark for anyone to see his boyish grin.

Again, he is staring at the back of her neck and notices her short blonde hair comes to a point, somewhat elfin. He can smell the scent of her perfume. Musky, not sweet. Sensual.

Jason says something funny, and Gia lets out a loud laugh and Jaime is caught up in her spell. She turns to look back at him and she smiles at him, her profile is in brief silhouette from a streetlight they pass by. It is just a flash, but he can carry that picture in his mind to bring up later just before he sleeps.

They arrive at The Biltmore and find a table for four. The ballroom is beautiful, loud, and alive with young patrons. A group of sailor's huddle at the bar, laughing and toasting while eyeing the young women that pass by them. They all enjoy a night far from the worries of war.

The dance floor is full and presents a colorful blur as the dancers' twirl around the floor, a happy cyclone warmed by the optimistic hopes of the young. This combination of courage, aspiration and American grit will fuel an army on an uphill march to victory.

As soon as they settle in, Tommy Miller grabs Gia's hand.

"Can't sit still through this song!" Tommy says as he leads her to the dance floor.

Jaime watches them with interest, and he is aware that a fair amount of jealousy has taken hold of him. He is surprised by this new emotion. It is something he has never experienced before. In a strange way, it is comforting. It confirms his newfound feelings for this interesting girl from Brooklyn. A smile has made its way to his handsome face once more.

Tommy is a confidant, handsome young man and boy can he dance. Tommy and Gia are dancing to 'Jumpin Jive' by Cab Calloway. Jaime smiles as he watches Gia, she is quite the dancer also. They are doing the Jitterbug and Tommy knows all the latest moves. He guides Gia with ease around the dance floor. The song ends and they weave their way through the crowd and back to the table.

"You're next!" Gia says to Jaime as she falls gracefully into the chair beside him. She gives him one of her breathtaking smiles. 'I'm a goner.' Jaime thinks.

Time stops and Jaime suddenly loves this table of four at the Biltmore. It is a moment to behold, to embrace and enjoy. Tomorrow is elusive, a mystery to all…given the uncertainty of war.

The evening is filled with music, dancing and daiquiris. Jaime grabs Gia's hand and leads her to the dance floor. They dance to 'God bless the Child' originally sung by Billie Holiday. Tonight, a local talent sings it and her voice is beautiful. The mirror ball, spinning on the ceiling, casts tiny sparkles on Gia's face and she is suddenly serious…….and she is suddenly beautiful…..and he is quite in love…..and he is still speechless, but it doesn't matter anymore. The music is enough. It is the last dance of the night.

They head home exhausted and quiet. Thoughts of war and uncertainty replace thoughts of youthful frivolity and innocent nights of play.

XI.   Cloudless Nights

The Chopmist Hill station will continue to intercept the tank-to-tank messages between Rommel and his troops. This allows the officials in Washington to alert British Intelligence of Rommel's movements in North Africa.

General Patton will also rely on the intercepted messages obtained by the Chopmist Hill Monitoring Station as the Americans battle their way through North Africa and on to Sicily. From these decisive battles forward, both Great Britain and the United States will rely significantly on the information gathered at the Chopmist Hill Station.

"Mr. Cave! I've tuned into a transmission coming from Germany again! Its regarding the weather reports coming out of Berlin! Looks like another cloudless night over Germany! A good night for the bomber pilots!" Tommy Miller alerts Thomas.

The British and American pilots will obtain information gathered at the Chopmist Hill station regarding the weather in the skies over Germany. The Chopmist Hill Station is able to pick up weather reports directly from Germany, something the British are unable to do. This astonishing reception allows the allies to properly plan successful night raids when the night skies are clear.

Jaime puts down his earphones and leans back and

stretches. It is time for a break. He swivels in his chair to face Gia's back. She is oblivious to everything around her, intent at the task at hand. He smiles at her intensity. She is frantically typing while listening to tapes, keys tapping out a wartime beat.

Suddenly she stops as if she is aware of Jaime's gaze. She swivels in her chair and they find themselves facing each other. They exchange smiles and then giggle for no apparent reason. Perhaps they already share a secret, and it makes them laugh. They like each other and believe that no one else has figured it out. But of course, they all have, the chemistry between the two of them is obvious. It's palpable in this small space shared by thirty people.

"It's a beautiful night out there. A cloudless night. Would you like to take a quick walk around the 'prison yard'?" Jaime suggests. The eight-foot-high chain link fence around the entire perimeter of the farm has prompted this nickname that all the listeners now share.

"Sure, lets stretch our legs. I've been hunched over and transcribing for most of the day. Some fresh air will do me good." Gia responds. The two leave the old farmhouse, suddenly aware of all the eyes following them out the front door.

Once again, Jaime is at a loss for words. He lets Gia lead the conversation.

"So how did you end up at this place?" Gia asks.

"I saw an ad in the Providence Journal. '*Wanted! Radio Operators to work for Uncle Sam!*', I've been an amateur radio buff since I was a kid, plus I speak fluent German. Just the right combination." Jaime replies with a smile.

"What about you?" he asks.

"Pretty much the same. I saw an ad in The Brooklyn Daily Eagle. My brother Joey and I had a ham radio, and he could take it apart and put it back together in no time flat! We would sit for hours listening in on different frequencies. He taught me all the ins and outs of radio maintenance and operation. I guess that was enough for the U.S. Civil Service and here I am! I also have exceptional typing skills. They even wavered the '5 years operator's license', because I did a pretty good job on the test they gave us! Looks like you and I were both recruited from the amateur ranks!" Gia says as they both laugh.

"What are you going to do when this crazy war is over?" she asks.

"I'll probably go back and finish my degree in engineering" he answers. "You?" he asks.

"Probably head back to Brooklyn and go to college." She replies.

"What's your major choice?" he asks.

"Something practical, a degree in fine arts. Just to be sure I will get a great high paying job when I finish." She replies and they both laugh. "But seriously, I do plan to concentrate on graphic design. So perhaps there is a lucrative career in my future after all." She adds.

"Ahhh an artist! I can see that. You look like an artist! Quirky!" He says and they both laugh. "You know, one of the best art schools in the county is right here in Rhode Island! The Rhode Island School of Design!" Jaime offers. Perhaps he can persuade her to stay on after the war, he thinks.

"So I've heard!" Gia responds with a smile.

They walk in silence for a long while. It is a beautiful cloudless summer night with a full moon. In the light of the moon, they both stop at the same time.

Up ahead, just outside the fence is a beautiful doe, she is nudging a tiny spotted fawn no more than a few weeks old. Gia and Jaime stand perfectly still and watch. The two are grazing and the mother lifts her head to look directly at them, but she doesn't move. She bends her head back down and continues chewing on the long-overgrown grass. As Jaime turns to Gia he notices she is wiping a tear away.

"Are you ok?" he asks

"I feel we have invaded their home with all this war time equipment. It makes me sad. I guess everything is getting to me lately. I'm worried about my brother Joey. He's in the army and has been sent to Europe. He's in Italy. We haven't heard from him in quite a while. No letters home." she replies.

"I'm sorry about that Gia." He says not knowing how to reassure her that all will be fine, when they both know that only time will tell. The reports coming out of Europe are grim, the Germans are occupying most of Europe. The casualties are extremely high.

They continue to walk, again in silence. Occasionally he glances over at her face lit up by the moon. It is a mixture of sadness, worry and exhaustion. But with all the strain these emotions might do to alter her young face, she still looks so beautiful to him. It is a face he would like to look at for a very long time to come.

They approach the old farmhouse, and he opens the door for her to pass through. The spell is broken by the sounds of the monitoring machines buzzing and humming capturing voices from far away.

XII. Crescent Park

Jaime sits at his station and catches up on his notes. He is transcribing onto index cards various clandestine radio transmissions and locations to be filed away for future reference. He takes a break and grabs one of the index cards and writes a message to Gia.

> *'Would you like to go dancing Friday night? Would you like to go to the 'Coney Island of the Northeast'? You'll feel right at home, like you're back in New York'.* —J

He drops the note at her station. She reads it and giggles, not really knowing what he is talking about. She has never heard of the place. She grabs one of her index cards and writes a simple Yes! And casually drops it on Jaime's desk.

On Friday night promptly at 7:00, Jaime pulls up in front of the farmhouse driving a jeep he has secured for the evening and waits. He is wearing a grey linen suit with a white button-down shirt. He has put on his best tie. He just purchased it at the Shepard's Department Store on Westminster Street in downtown Providence. It has a geometric design of blue, black, and grey with tiny dashes of lime green.

He has also purchased a pair of pale pink mesh gloves with matching pink embroidery around the wrist for Gia. They have a pearl button to fasten them just above the wrist. He smiles to himself thinking about the hour he spent with the salesclerk trying to decide on the right pair. She was nice enough to lay out six pairs on the counter…..and then six more.

"Pink it is!" He says finally. "Perfect!" the salesgirl replies with a sigh of relief. She then boxes and gift wraps them in black and silver striped tissue paper tied with a pink satin ribbon.

"She will love them!" she adds with a smile, grateful a decision has finally been made.

Gia opens the screen door and walks out onto the porch. She is wearing a white halter dress that fits her snuggly down to her hips and then flairs. Her sandals are high and strappy, coral pattern leather. She wears round sunglasses low on her nose, a big smile on her face. Summer pink lipstick.

Perfect, he thinks to himself. The gloves will match her smiling lips. She saunters down the steps and jumps in. He gives her the most casual hello he can fake. God, he thinks, let me be somewhat cool with this girl. She is sending his world into a spin that is as unnerving as it is exciting.

Before they settle in for the ride he nervously passes her the box. "Something to match your lipstick" he says. She hurriedly opens the box as a child would on Christmas morning.

"Oh my! They are lovely!". She slides them on, and

they fit perfectly snug. She holds up her hands to admire them. He's relieved and happy at the same time as he can tell she truly loves them.

"Thank you Jaime! They are perfect!" she adds as she leans in to kiss his cheek. He slowly pulls out of the driveway trying, with no success, to suppress the big grin that has formed on his face.

They drive through the farmlands of Scituate and Johnston heading east through Providence and then they travel down a long road on the east side of Narragansett Bay. In the early evening light, the bay water sparkles from the angle of the sun. There are fields of farmland that stretch from the road to the bay. Some are spotted with cows and horses grazing as evening approaches.

Then they pass the shoreline of the bay where small beach cottages have sprouted up over the years to form a seaside community. They are built close together, most with wrap around porches facing the water. The cottages are built along the train route. They provide affordable summer get-away's with quick and easy access from Providence and Massachusetts.

Jaime is pleased with his choice of a 'first date' destination. He knows it will brighten Gia's spirits. Growing up in Rhode Island, Crescent Park of Riverside, has always been one of his favorite places to visit. Jaime and his friends would venture to the park several times every summer. They would take in all the rides, have a shore dinner of fresh local seafood, and eat taffy and cotton candy. In addition to the rides, there is a beautiful ballroom called The Alhambra.

As they round the last corner, Crescent Park comes into view. Colorful lights illuminate the early evening sky. They can hear the music and excited laughter of both children and adults. They can smell the unmistakable scent of frying doughboy fritters in the air. It is a magical place where the worry of the times is replaced with the carefree joys of childhood.

"First stop is the carousel." Jaime says. He gathers up every nerve in his body and grabs her gloved hand. Their hurried walk almost turns into a run as they approach the park. They are both caught up in the enchantment of the place.

Gia is speechless, it is just like Coney Island. Her parents would take her and her brother Joey to Coney Island every August as a special treat just before going back to school in September. She remembers running hand in hand with her brother from ride to ride. Her father would help them both at a game so they could win a prize, usually a stuffed animal. The collection of stuffed animals still line her bedroom shelves at home.

She is suddenly feeling nostalgic and homesick. She misses her parents and her brother Joey so much. Taking this job in Rhode Island is the first time she has been away from them for an extended amount of time.

She realizes her feeling of nostalgia is mixed with something new, something exciting and comforting at the same time……she holds on to Jaime's hand a little bit tighter.

The carousel slows for the next group of eager riders. Gia gazes at the carousel in awe. It is an original Looff carousel built in 1895. The beautifully painted horses move up and down slowly at first and then the ride picks up speed. The pipe organ in the middle is surrounded by little painted cherubs playing trumpets, it plays loudly. Riders on the outside horses reach for suspended brass rings and throw them into a wooden clown's mouth.

As they ride the carousel Jaime glances over at Gia. She is laughing and the stresses of war have left her face. They are replaced with the look of childhood wonder. Jaime feels confident for the first time in her presence and laughs as he grabs a brass ring and tosses it cleanly into the wooden clown's mouth.

They walk all through the park, eating every 'fried morsel' they can find. They take in a few of the rides as they go. The haunted house is Jaime's favorite because as she screams he leans into her to hold her and give her a kiss on the cheek. Once again he can smell the scent of her perfume.

They end the night at the Alhambra ballroom. As they enter the hall, they are both transfixed by its beauty. It is a stunning art deco hall with the most enormous red crystal chandeliers Gia has ever seen. The mahogany floors are highly polished, and the dancers make their way around the room.

A big band plays, each musician sits behind a white painted box with a large letter A for Alhambra painted on the front. The band plays Glen Miller, Count Basie and Tommy Dorsey songs as the dancers do the fox-trot, gliding gracefully as they go by.

Jaime takes Gia by the hand and walks her unto the

dance floor. Glen Millers 'In the Mood' is playing. The perfect song. The perfect night. The perfect girl.

He tightens his arm around her waist and effortlessly leads her around the floor. They make a lovely pair, and he is elated to observe that some of the patrons are watching the two of them with interest as they dance. Perhaps they already know that these two are falling in love.

Pangs of new love carry pangs of doubt. He wonders if he will ever have a better night than this one. So he pulls her in a little closer just in case.

XIII.   Ships & U–Boats

As Jaime sits at his post at the station, he hears cryptic messages clearly in German, but the transmissions are coming out of South America. He zooms in on Brazil.

Over and over, he hears mention of 'The Queen Mary' mixed with harsh tones of the German language. He calls Thomas over to listen in. The transmission is scratchy.

"Sounds like it is coming from a U-Boat or a clandestine station on land." Jamie says to Thomas.

"Yes, could be off the coast of Brazil....or land, hard to decipher exact location. If it's a U-boat, it is awfully close to land." Thomas says confirming Jaime's suspicions.

The listeners are also able to locate the exact locations of German U-boats. In the onset of the war, many are successful in sinking allied cargo ships crossing the Atlantic. When the United States enters the war in 1941, the U-Boats begin to swarm the Eastern seaboard.

Jamie and Thomas both wonder if perhaps the Germans have been able to track the route of the ship. The U-boat could be on its way to take out the Queen Mary.

"Jaime, The Queen Mary is assisting in the war effort. She's been outfitted for transport! Jesus, she's probably carrying thousands of troops as we speak! Let's prioritize and get this message down to D.C.!" Thomas informs Jaime.

Within hours, Thomas hears back. He walks back and leans over to let Jaime know the outcome of the interception.

"Apparently, the ship had just left Rio de Janeiro carrying close to fourteen thousand allied troops to Australia. Good work Jaime, damn good work. They were able to alert the Brits who in turn informed the captain so he could alter his route. They were successful in preventing what could have been a catastrophe for all the troops on board." Thomas says as he pats Jaime on the shoulder.

XIV.   Jaime's Mission

One Monday afternoon in early March of 1944, Gia stands on the front porch of the farmhouse having her daily cigarette. Its early evening, the sun is beginning to set. It's a cold day and the winter's-end wind is picking up as the night descends on them. The wind carries the ashes from the tip of her cigarette, and they float into the dusk sky, some are still alight. She watches them drift away and disappear, reminding her of fireflies. She pulls the old cardigan she is wearing tighter around her to keep away the cold.

She glances out toward the barracks where the men are staying. She notices Thomas and Jaime are standing outside and appear to be in a very deep and serious conversation. Jaime's brows are furrowed, and he looks worried. The worry he is feeling slowly makes its way toward the porch and settles inside her. 'Something is going on' Gia thinks, and she doesn't like the feel of it.

He lifts his head to look toward the porch. He sees Gia and smiles as if attempting to put Gia at ease, but she can tell that his smile is masking a very different emotion. There's a mixture of sadness and concern behind his smile. Thomas and Jaime chat for some time and then they wrap up their conversation. Thomas walks away briskly and passes Gia on the porch. He gives her a forced and obligatory smile, but he doesn't say a word. Gia realizes her intuition is correct. Something is awry.

Jaime takes his time and strides slowly toward the porch. Gia surmises he is gathering his thoughts. She stubs out her cigarette, vowing to quit completely when this god-forsaken war is over.

"Up for a cocktail at the tavern in Chepachet?" Jaime asks Gia. When they want to stay local, they go to 'The Tavern on Main' located in the neighboring village of Chepachet, Jaime's hometown. The Tavern on the Main, built in the late 1700's, is one of the oldest running taverns in Rhode Island.

"Sure." replies Gia, trying to keep it light. She knows something is off with Jaime. He is obviously distracted by something.

During the drive over to the tavern, Gia tries to engage Jaime in conversation. But he remains silent. He reaches to hold her hand as they drive. It calms and stills her racing mind. She wishes he would blurt out whatever it is he is holding in. The silence is awkward and creates tension.

They settle into a cozy booth. The fireplace is lit, and they can feel its warmth from where they sit. The red leather seats are cracked with age. The oak table carries the scars of over a hundred years of good use.

He sits across from her, and then decides he'd rather sit next to her, feel her shoulders against him. She moves over to oblige him. He takes her hand again.

"They are sending me to London." He says, not able to keep it in any longer. She tries so hard to hide her

disappointment and her fears. She tries to appear nonchalant but worry shows on her face. She attempts to keep a
smile on her face in spite of what he is telling her, but it is
too hard to maintain.

"They are sending me to work on a 'double-cross' spy
system prior to the Allied invasion of occupied France."
All the listeners are now fully aware of the imminent
invasion of Nazi occupied Europe by the allies. Although
it is top secret, they have been informed so they can mon-
itor any transmitted messages that may alert the Nazi's of
the planned destination and date of the invasion.

"I cannot go into detail with you, as you know." says
Jaime.

The mission involves convincing the German spies
in London that the allied invasion of France will happen
in Calais and Norway, not Normandy. German agents
have parachuted onto English soil, others have come by
boat. The majority have been tracked down and captured
immediately. The rest have infiltrated London, some are
hiding in plain sight. They are blending in with the citizens of London.

Some of the German spies have carried suitcases into
London fitted with shortwave radio equipment used for
transmitting crucial war information back to Germany.

Because Jaime is familiar with locating clandestine radio's and is fluent in German, he is being sent to
London. His perfect Berlin accent will further convince
the enemy of his loyalty to The Third Reich. His mission in London will involve working side by side with the
British Security Service known as M15.

His instructions will come from another double-cross agent who has been working for the agency since 1939. The German sympathizers and spies believe that they are informing the Nazi Intelligence Agency, known as Abwehr, of classified war information only known by British Intelligence. In fact, they will be delivering convoluted messages that contain false information regarding the war strategy and movements of the allies.

Of course Gia realizes the dangers Jaime will be facing and so does he. London is still recovering from the blitz; the bombing was relentless over the city of London from 1940-41. Although they are rebuilding the historic city, they know it is just a matter of time before the Germans will return for another bombardment and possible invasion.

Jaime and Gia sit in silence for a while. She holds his hand tighter. The gin warms her stomach and slightly numbs her senses and her fears seem misted somewhat by the alcohol.

"When are you leaving?" She asks, not really wanting the answer. "Thursday." He replies. "Let's have a proper sendoff Wednesday night?" he says. "Let's go for a fancy dinner and then dancing at the Biltmore." He adds. They drive home in silence, lost in their own thoughts. Holding hands seems enough.

XV.   Stormy Weather

On Wednesday night Jaime dresses in his best suit and tie. He is nervous, excited and sad all at the same time. His future is now so unsure. He is leaving the security and safety of a job on the domestic front and heading into the volatile war zone. He is leaving home, his parents. He is leaving the girl he has fallen in love with.

Gia has put on her very best dress. Her mother sent it to her for her birthday. It is a tight fitting deep red halter dress of heavy textured silk. It falls just below her knees. She wears black silk pumps and black jet crystal pearl-drop earrings. The darkest red lipstick she can find. Her hand trembles as she applies it. She too has fallen in love and the thought of Jaime leaving has left her shaken.

As they take the ride to Providence they are both quiet, alone in their own thoughts of inevitable separation. Jaime surprises Gia with the restaurant choice. He pulls up in front of Camille's restaurant on Federal Hill in Providence, the little Italy of Rhode Island.

"I thought you could use a really great Italian meal." Jaime says as the valet opens the door on her side. "Just like home. Just like Brooklyn." He adds. Gia is once again caught off guard by Jaime and his thoughtful little surprises that he plans just for her. She looks at him and smiles and this time, she is the one left speechless.

Jaime and Gia enjoy a delicious meal together. It is the best Gia has had since she arrived in Rhode Island. The food tastes as good as her moms and she feels right at home dipping the home baked Italian bread into the spicy tomato 'gravy'. They share a straw wrapped bottle of Chianti while sitting in a candle lit booth nestled in the corner.

Next stop is the Biltmore. When they arrive and surround themselves with the other young dancers they soon find they are laughing and enjoying a much-needed distraction from their worries.

After a few dances, they settle into a table in the corner. The table is dressed in white and cream, white tablecloth with a low cream vase of white roses. They sit next to each other, not across, so they can watch the dancers and the big band. He orders two glasses of champagne and chocolate cake.

He reaches for her chair and pulls her closer to him and puts his arm around her shoulder. "I will be back before you know it" he says to reassure her.

"Just be safe Jaime, keep yourself safe. It's a whole different world over there." she says. He nods and tightens his grip around her bare shoulders.

'Sing Sing Sing' by Benny Goodman is being played by the Biltmore big band and they can't stay seated. The beat calls them back to the dance floor. The song is followed by 'It don't mean a thing.' by Duke Ellington.

They dance to the last song of the night 'Stormy Weather' by Lena Horne.....a clear message of things to come. They dance slower than the other dancers, holding each other almost motionless as if to stop time. If they could, they would remain this way and forever drift in this beautiful ballroom at the Biltmore. But wartime duties call. The spell is broken when the last note of music is played.

It's been a long and wonderful night and it's time to head home. Again, they drive home in silence both exhausted and dreading the next day.

Jaime and Gia sit on the front porch steps of the farmhouse not wanting the night to end. He runs to the barracks and grabs a bottle of gin and a blanket to wrap around them, they both sip from it enjoying its numbing affect. In between the sips they kiss. The kisses are long and lingering.

As they kiss, Gia slips something into Jaime's hand. He looks down and sees a small silver charm. It is in the shape of the North Star. He flips it over and on the back it says, 'To find your way home'.

"Keep it with you and think of me in London. My mother gave it to me when I left Brooklyn to come here. The north star is one of the brightest stars in the sky and it will guide you home." Gia says.

"I will carry it always." Jaime responds as he buries it in his pocket.

He pulls her closer and whispers in her ear "Marry me when I come home." Her next kiss gives him the answer. They both return to their beds exhausted. They spend a sleepless night, tossing and turning.....thoughts of love mingle with thoughts of war and the uncertainty of things to come.

XVI.   Union Station

Jaime is up early and ready to go, he is taking the train from Providence to New York to fly to London. Gia offers to drive him there and Thomas relents with a smile knowing that these two have something heavy going on. They all gather to wish Jaime well before he leaves Chopmist Hill.

Gia stands with him at the train platform, they hug for what seems an eternity and at the same time it's just too brief. He boards the train, waving from the first window he can find......and then he is gone.

She stands there for a while, even though the train is long gone. She feels lost in a world that holds no certainty for her anymore. Will the Allies succeed? Will the Germans invade the United States? Will Jaime come home soon? Where is her brother Joey? What has happened to him and why hasn't he written?

Nothing is certain anymore, for anyone. She drives back to Chopmist Hill more determined than ever to carry on intercepting the messages that will help defeat the enemy that lurks at their doorstep. She does this while anxiously awaiting Jaime and Joey's safe return.

XVII.   Going Home

Gia is sitting at her station in late May, just a few weeks before D-Day when she is handed a letter from home. She opens it and reads.

Ciao My Dear Gia,

> *Your mother and I miss you dearly. It has been too long since your last visit. I was wondering if you could make a trip home for a few days. I realize you are very busy with your job, but I would like to surprise your Mom. Please let me know when you can arrange to visit.*

> *Your loving Papa.*

Gia leans back in her chair and runs her fingers through her hair. She realizes she hasn't visited home since Christmas. Five months...How did the time get away from her? Her mother has been worried sick about her brother Joey, they still have not heard from him. Gia is suddenly gripped with sadness and guilt. She has been so wrapped up with Jaime and her job in Rhode Island, she has allowed too much time go by since her last visit home.

She immediately excuses herself to call home. After

a conversation with her mother, she asks to talk to her father. Without her mother's knowledge, she tells her father that of course she will come home. She has the following weekend off. He arranges to pick her up at Grand Central Station on Friday night.

Gia departs Union Station in Providence on the following Friday afternoon. She is excited to see her parents. She settles into a comfortable seat and falls asleep on the way to New York. She can vaguely hear the calls for each stop along the way. Between stops she is gently lulled to sleep again. It is the first fitful sleep she has had in months.

'*Going home. Going home.*' By Antonin Dvorzak, the old hymn plays in her mind over and over again as she sleeps, much like a lullaby.

"GRAND CENTRAL! GRAND CENTRAL! NEXT STOP GRAND CENTRAL STATION NEW YORK CITY! FINAL DESTINATION! WELCOME TO NEW YORK!"

Gia awakens with a start; it is the loudest call she has heard on the entire journey home. Still half asleep, she fumbles trying to grab her overnight bag from the overhead compartment. She makes her way to the front of the train car to disembark. The train lurches to a stop and she is thrown off balance leaning into the woman standing next to her. Finally, she rights herself and they all disembark.

As she steps off the train she tries to locate her father as she winds her way through the crowd of weary travelers.

She has to stand on tiptoes to see as she weaves her way through.

Up ahead she notices a young man on crutches making his way toward her. His head is tilted down as he struggles with his new apparatus. Most certainly a war injury, Gia concludes. As he gets closer his face slowly tilts up, Gia feels the tears of joy and relief spring from her eyes. Her little brother….Joey and his beautiful smiling face making his way towards her.

"Joey! Joey! Thank God Joey!" she yells as she runs toward her little brother, tears streaming down her face.

"Surprise! Surprise! A little bit of shrapnel and I'm home!" Joey says.

Gia is so overwhelmed she suddenly feels light-headed and giddy. As she hugs him, she looks beyond and there just behind him stands her mother and father both in tears. They were the ones to surprise her! They are together again, just the four of them!

Joey was injured in the battle at Monte Cassino, Italy. "Close to the village where Mama and Papa were born." Joey says proudly.

The injury to his leg is bad. His knee is shattered. "I'm home for good Gia, my days as a soldier are over! So is my dream of a career in baseball." He says kiddingly. As a kid Joey had dreams of playing for The Brooklyn Dodgers. Joey and Gia would jump the fence at Ebbets Field to watch the team practice.

Gia can see that this injury is a life changer for Joey. He will walk with a limp for the rest of his life. It will be a constant reminder of the war and the battles he fought.

A reminder of the friends he lost. Yet Joey will consider himself one of the lucky ones. He made it home.

Gia notices that in spite of Joey's new injury he is quite elated and jovial.

"Joey, I know this lovely glow on your face cannot be just for me. What's up with you, little brother?" She asks glancing sideways at him. She sees he is trying to act cool and collected, but his face reveals something in opposition to that. It's as if he is keeping a beautiful secret that he cannot wait to reveal to her.

"I've met a girl! Her name is Gabrielle. She lives with her aunt and uncle in our building. She came all the way from Paris. She's perfect, absolutely perfect." He says. Gia has never seen her little brother like this. She realizes that he is in love, completely in love. " I can't wait for you to meet her!" he adds.

On their way back to Brooklyn, Joey tells Gia about Gabrielle. She left Paris a few months after the Nazi's marched into the city in June of 1940. Being Jewish, she made a treacherous journey out of Paris in the middle of the night with the help of an underground network arranged by a wealthy American. First arriving in Lisbon, she boarded a Pan American Clipper plane, along with other refugees, destined for New York City. She now lives with relatives in the apartment just below theirs. She had to leave her mother behind. Her father is a French prisoner of war being held in a German camp. She has not heard from her mother since she left.

Joey also explains how they met. One afternoon as he struggled to get up the stairs on his crutches, Gabrielle offered to help him. They ended up spending two hours in the hallway, sitting on the stairs, talking. Her mix of two languages intoxicated Joey. Before long, he understood her perfectly….. and she understood him. It was meant to be, this girl from Paris ending up in a stairwell in Brooklyn in deep conversation with the boy who lives upstairs. They soon became inseparable.

"She is in her first year at Brooklyn College, studying journalism. She's a wonderful writer! I fell for her in an instant. Since then, I have seen her every day. She has met Mama and Papa and they love her. I know you will too Gia. I'm sure of it!" Joey says with a big grin on his face.

On Gia's second night home, Joey disappears. He hobbles out the door and returns a half hour later with Gabrielle. Joey has brought her to dinner to meet Gia. Gia can see why Joey has fallen for this girl. She is lovely. She struggles with the English language a bit, but she is smart and already has a remarkable command of it. Her French accent adds to her exotic beauty.

Gia watches the two of them with interest. The way they look at each other, the way he reaches for her hand, the air that surrounds them. Every single element points to love. Gia knows this because it has happened to her.

After a while Gia settles in on the couch next to Gabrielle. They quickly adapt to the language barrier and their conversation starts to flow. They are soon in deep conversation. Gia learns about Gabrielle's life in Paris and her treacherous journey to America.

Gia is fascinated by Gabrielle's story. She is a courageous and intelligent young woman. She is also quick witted, and Gia understands why Joey is so enthralled with her. Gia and Gabrielle are soon giggling together. Gia is so happy Joey has found her. She is so happy they have found each-other.

Gia spends four glorious days with her family, which now includes Gabrielle. They visit all of her favorite haunts, including Totonno Pizzeria Napolitana for the best pizza in Brooklyn. Her mother will make all of the favorite dishes of their childhood, including Gia's two favorite's spaghetti and meatballs and fried smelts.

Joey and Gabrielle take Gia to Grand Central Station, when it is time for her to make the journey back to Rhode Island.

"See you soon sis!" Joey says as Gia boards the train.

"Avoir un bon voyage!" Gabrielle says to Gia as she leans in to kiss her on both cheeks. Gia pulls her in for a big hug.

When Gia settles in her seat, she reflects on her visit home to Brooklyn. She is so relieved that her brother is finally home and out of harm's way. He has fallen in love with quite an interesting young woman. Gia smiles. Imagine, she thinks. Her little brother in love with a Parisian girl…..and a journalism major! Gia can see the determination in Gabrielle's eyes. She will succeed in whatever she puts her mind to.

XVIII. Gabrielle in Paris 1940

G abrielle Blum and her mother Joelle stand with the small crowd on the Champ Élyées. Since the mass exodus of Parisians ahead of the German occupation, the streets are mostly empty. Gabrielle and Joelle have ventured out to witness the Germans make their first appearance in their beloved city.

Joelle has somehow convinced herself that she must witness the soldiers marching in. And in doing so, she will be able to determine their mind set. She will be able to ascertain whether it will be a 'friendly take-over' as promised by studying their faces as they walk by.

They can hear the stomping boots of the German soldiers as they approach the Arc de Triomphe. It is a sad and frightening day for the Parisians. No one thought the day would come. Paris has fallen to the Nazi's. The fighting has ended far from the city, so the Nazi's march into Paris without any resistance.

The crowd is quiet, solemn. There is nothing to celebrate. The fear is palpable. It is no secret to the Jewish citizens living in Paris that the Nazi's are not tolerant of them. The rumors swirl of the horrors taking place in Germany, Poland, Austria and all of the other countries that have fallen to the Nazi's. They are rounding up Jews and sending them to work camps, never to return. They simply disappear. Despite the rumors, some of the Parisians mistakenly believe they will not suffer the same fate.

Gabrielle and her mother have remained in Paris, they have nowhere else to go. Besides, Joelle has to run her dress shop located in a neighborhood on the left bank to make a living to support them. It is just the two of them now. Gabrielle's father Philip was a tailor, taking care of the men's side of the shop. Now Joelle can only keep up with the dressmaking for her lady clients.

Philip joined the French army in 1939. When the French were defeated by the Germans, he was taken as a prisoner of war. They have had no contact with him, they don't know if he is dead or alive.

Now Joelle regrets her decision not to leave the city regardless of not having secured a place to stay outside of Paris. She is not certain she and Gabrielle will be allowed to go anywhere now. A gripping fear takes hold of her.

The soldiers start their march under the Arc de Triomphe and along the Champs Élysées. They pass right in front of Gabrielle and Joelle. It is an unnerving sight to behold. The crowd watches in disbelief, many with tears rolling unchecked down their faces. Most of the tears come from the older veterans of the Great War, the ones who fought so hard to defeat the Germans. Now here they are, marching into Paris without any resistance at all.

Joelle studies the faces of the soldiers as they march past, and she does not like what she sees. The vacant and cold look in their eyes unnerves her. It chills her to the bone, even on this hot day in June. They stare straight ahead and march with marked precision, as if they are one.

Joelle realizes that their way of life, to live free in the enlightened city of Paris, is gone. The city of light has gone dark.

As Gabrielle and Joelle make their way back to the left bank, it is evident how the city has been affected on this historic day. Paris is silent. Even on the busiest avenue, no one is speaking. The whole city is silent, as if they are all in mourning. And, of course, they are.

XIX. La Rive Gauche

Gabrielle and Joelle return to their normal routine in the days following the German's march into Paris. At first, Joelle feels relieved. Nothing much appears to have changed since the occupation. Many believe the false propaganda that has been spread throughout the city by the Nazi's that Paris will remain the same. That the citizens of Paris will be left alone, to carry on as they always have.

Joelle oversees her dress shop. She orders the best fabric, designs the most beautiful dresses, and sells them to her long list of clients. Gabrielle attends school, studying hard so she can eventually attend university to become a journalist.

By August, Joelle has noticed a steady decline in her customers. Some make excuses as to why they cannot buy from her any longer, some just stop coming all-together. Business is only done with her most loyal customers.

The Germans have issued rations on most everything. Lines now form for even the staple items, including bread. Things have started to change, and life will become harder and harder for the Parisian's. It will become a life-or-death situation for the Parisian Jews.

At first it is understood that Paris will not change. It

is understood that the Jewish population living in Paris will be left alone. But it is only misleading publicity to ensure the citizens of Paris remain calm. It is to encourage a feeling of well-being and safety. A pretense that will start to unravel and once it starts to unravel it will gain momentum quickly.

XX.   Saving Gabrielle

Joelle worries for Gabrielle, and she starts to consider different options to get her out of Paris and to safety. With or without her, she will somehow find a way to get Gabrielle to safety.

One afternoon in mid-September, Joelle and her close friend Camille enjoy an afternoon tea in Joelle's apartment above her shop. Joelle sets down the tray carrying the tea, lemon, and sugar cubes in her best bone china tea service. In addition, is Rugelach. Joelle knows these are Camille's favorite pastries.

Lemons are a rarity during the occupation, so Joelle is thrilled when Camille takes one out of her dress pocket and tosses it to Joelle when she first arrives. They both giggle as Joelle tosses it back and they play a spontaneous game of catch. Joelle realizes it's the first time she has laughed in quite some time. She is so consumed with worry and fear.

"There are some options we can consider to get Gabrielle to safety. I am hearing that Jewish citizens will have to register by late October." Camille says. "We must act now before it's too late. You also have to consider yourself Joelle. Paris is no longer safe for you as well." She adds.

"One option is to obtain counterfeit passports and try to get you both to Spain or Portugal. From there you can get to America. They can be pricey and the journey dangerous if you are discovered at the border without convincing papers. You could face arrest or even worse, so I have heard!" Camille says. "We would have to secure the passports from the very best forger Paris has to offer. I think it is much too risky at this point." She adds.

"I am more concerned for Gabrielle than me right now. I have relatives in Brooklyn, New York.....my cousin. If I can somehow get her out of France, she has a family that will take her in. She can continue her education." says Joelle. "Let me know if you hear of any safe passage for her. I can stay behind and keep the dress shop going until the war ends. I need to be here when Philip returns." Joelle adds.

"Joelle, I think you are being a bit too optimistic about staying in Paris. It's time to get out while there still may be a chance. Perhaps you should go south to the unoccupied zone. I can alert Philip when he returns of your decision to leave and where he can find you." Camille says as she wonders if Philip will ever return. Camille knows that the prison camps are harsh. Men are dying of decease and starvation. Some have died from injuries incurred while in battle and even torture.

They sit and discuss the changes that have occurred in Paris since the Nazi's have marched in. It has only been two and a half months, yet their entire world has changed dramatically. They both try to keep the conversation light-hearted as they sip their tea. They both long for the old days of afternoon visits together, when their worries were minor and inconsequential. When their laughter filled the room. In comparison, now their worries include momentous decisions. Some regarding life itself.

"I will let you know of any news I hear of safe passage for you and Gabrielle." Camille says as she kisses Joelle's cheek and leaves. Camille stands on the landing and leans against the closed door of her best friend's apartment. She lets out a heavy sigh. What will happen to Joelle and Gabrielle, she wonders? How can she help them?

XXI. The Conversation

"**G**abrielle, come sit at the table and have a cup of tea. Camille brought another lemon today and I saved half of it to squeeze into our tea." Joelle says to her daughter.

Joelle places a small plate of rugelach on the table. She sits across from her daughter. Gabrielle has stopped going to school, so she is continuing her studies at home. Jews are no longer allowed to attend school in Paris.

"Gabrielle, I know you realize that we are in grave danger. I have contacted my cousin Samuel in Brooklyn, New York in America. His wife Martine is there also, with their daughter Chloe. You can go to school there, finish your studies and go on to university. I am telling you now, that you must go there for your own safety. I will remain here and wait for your Papa's return and then we will join you there." Joelle says sternly, holding back the inevitable tears.

"Mama don't be silly. You know I would never leave without you." Gabrielle replies. "We will be fine. I can do my studies at home. The war will eventually end, and everything will go back to normal. We will stay here together and wait for Papa," she adds.

Joelle looks into her daughters' beautiful blue eyes.

They are the eyes of a hopeful girl with her whole life in front of her. And that is why Joelle maintains her stern demeanor. Her daughter must leave without her.

A few days prior to this conversation. Joelle finds a note tucked under her door.

Joelle, bring Gabrielle to Le Bristol Hotel on November 5th at midnight. We have secured false papers and passage for her. Pack a small traveling bag. Her journey will take her to New York.

The note holds no signature, but Joelle suspects Camille is behind the plan to save her daughter and for safety reasons she has withheld her signature.

XXII.   November 5th, 1940

Gabrielle and Joelle sleep in the same bed. They have done so since the Nazi's marched in five months ago. They wake up the morning of the 5th at the same time. They lay there in silence for a long time, staring at each other.

Joelle reaches over to grab Gabrielle's hand and the inevitable tears begin to flow from both of them. So much is going through Joelle's mind. Will I ever see my daughter again? Will she make it to New York safely? How will I know she has made it there? How will I get to her after the war? There are too many questions that hold her on the brink of collapse.

She must push them aside and get through this day. She must get Gabrielle safely to Le Bristol in the middle of the night. She must do this even though curfews have been put in place. If they are caught they will both be imprisoned, perhaps even sent away or killed on the spot.

They spend the day together in the apartment. Joelle puts aside her work for the day. Her dressmaking has diminished significantly in the past few months. Her dress shop is mostly closed now. Her clients come to the apartment, and she works from there. It is safer for her to do her business under the radar of the Nazi soldiers patrolling the neighborhood. Signs are now required on all Jewish businesses stating that the business is owned by a Jew.

Gabrielle sits on the sofa as Joelle packs her small suitcase for the journey. She packs her three finest dresses, two skirts, two blouses, undergarments and toiletries only found in Paris.

In between the garments she tucks some of their most valuable pieces. Silver and gold jewelry including Joelle's engagement and wedding ring are tucked within the clothing. A silver sugar bowl and creamer and tiny Saint Louis crystal vase given to Joelle by her mother on the eve of her wedding to Philip are included. Joelle also gives Gabrielle a small amount of cash that she has saved. She tells Gabrielle to give the money to Cousin Samuel to help with the costs of providing her with a home. If she needs extra money, she is to sell the items that Joelle has packed for the journey.

The last piece she packs is a photograph in a silver art nouveau frame. It is a photograph of the three of them, Philip, Joelle, and Gabrielle. A family of three, smiling and at ease picnicking on the banks of the Seine one summer day years ago. Joelle wraps it in a silk scarf Philip gave her for their first wedding anniversary. Her perfume still lingers on it…..it will linger there for years to come.

They sit together well into the evening. The plan is to start to make their way to Le Bristol at 11:00. It could take them at least an hour to walk there, as they try to remain out of sight the entire way.

It is 10:30 when they hear a soft knock on the door. Joelle motions Gabrielle to keep quiet by raising her finger to her lips. She removes her shoes and walks silently to the door.

Her heart is pounding. What if someone has found out? What if someone has turned them in? All these thoughts go through Joelle's mind as she walks toward the door.

"Joelle, its Camille. Open the door." Says Camille to Joelle's relief. Joelle slowly opens the door to peak out and Camille is standing there with her husband Pierre. Joelle opens the door, and they quickly scurry inside.

"Change of plans, Joelle! We will be taking Gabrielle to Le Bristol. It is not safe for you or Gabrielle. If they stop you, they will take you both to God knows where. People are disappearing Joelle. Jews are disappearing. If we get stopped, we are simply out making our way home after a late dinner at the Ritz with our daughter. We dressed for the occasion. Pierre frequents the bar at the Ritz, so he is known there. He will be vouched for if it comes to that." explains Camille.

"I knew it was you Camille. How can I ever thank you!" exclaims Joelle.

"Make me one of those beautiful dresses of yours!" replies Camille. "We'll show the Nazi bastards how the true Parisians dress". She adds. They all laugh, but the laughter fades as quickly as it starts. It is extinguished by the heartbreaking reality of the moment.

"Who is taking her to America? Who is at Le Bristol and what is the plan? How do I know she will be safe?" Joelle asks.

"I will come back tomorrow and explain the whole plan. For now, you must trust me Joelle. This is the safest way. We must leave now. It is time to say goodbye. We will wait at the front door." Camille says.

Joelle takes Gabrielle's hand and motions her to sit on the couch beside her. Gabrielle starts to sob uncontrollably.

"Gabrielle, you must be brave. You must get to safety now. I will follow. I will find you. I Promise I will do everything in my power to get to you as soon as I can. When you arrive in New York safely you must write to Camille to let her know you have arrived. The Nazi's are censoring the letters coming in and going out of Paris that are being sent by Jews and to Jews. Use Camille's' last name on the envelope. It is no longer safe to write to me. I will write back through Camille. I love you more than life itself and I know you know that. Do this for us Gabrielle. Get to safety now!" Joelle says while holding back her tears. They embrace each other so tightly it is hard to breath. Joelle gently loosens the grip she has on her daughter and leads her to the door.

"Here is the address of cousin Samuel. Tuck it safely, do not show anyone. When you get to New York, you must find your way to his home. I have written in English how you can ask for directions when you arrive in New York. Be brave, mon amour. " Joelle says as she holds her tight one more time.

And then she is gone. Her Gabrielle is gone. Joelle is fully aware that she may never see her daughter again. But Joelle's love for Gabrielle and her yearning to get her to safety overpowers her need to keep her close. She falls onto the couch and lets the tears flow until there are none left to fall. In the early hours of the next morning as the sun is casting its first light, she finally drifts off to sleep.

She dreams of Gabrielle, she is a little girl sitting on

the banks of the Seine eating her favorite piece of fruit, an apricot. She is only six years old. She sits on a plaid blanket with her parents. A stranger walking by offers to take their picture. They pass their camera to him. He is the witness to their happiness on a sunny day so long ago.

XXIII.   A Change of Heart

Joelle sleeps on and off throughout the morning. She would rather be asleep than awake in a world without her daughter there next to her, so she allows herself to continue sleeping in hopes that her dreams will take her away from the world she is now faced with.

When she finally shakes off the sleep, reality hits her like a brick flying across the room. 'What have I done!' she thinks. 'I need to get her back!' Joelle dresses in a panic. She straightens her hair wave to look freshly done. She applies lipstick with a shaky hand. As she gets ready, she contemplates what might be the quickest route she can take by foot to Le Bristol. She runs out her door and down the stairs to street level. She opens the door and runs straight into Camille who has her hand on the outside doorknob.

"Camille!" Joelle sobs. "I need to get her back! Please help me get her back! I've changed my mind; she needs to be with me!" she shouts at Camille.

Camille grabs Joelle by the arm and tightens her squeeze to the point of pain.

"Listen to me." Camille says in a hushed tone full of tense warning. "You need to pull yourself together, turn yourself around and go back upstairs with me before you draw any attention to yourself. I will explain everything to you. Now let's get inside!" Camille adds.

Camille glances across the street and she notices Claudette Garnier, the owner of a hair salon both Camille and Joelle frequent, is standing in front of her shop talking to a German officer. Claudette then turns and notices Camille and Joelle and her smile turns into an unbecoming sneer.

Camille pretends not to see her and guides Joelle back through the door. When she sneaks a look back, she notices Claudette has turned her attention back to the officer and is clearly flirting with him and he is flirting back.

Traitor, Camille thinks. Camille hopes that Claudette will get hers when the war is over for engaging with the enemy and turning on her own people. Camille makes a note that Joelle must be made aware that Claudette now poses a threat because of the company she keeps. Camille realizes that she must now devise a plan to get Joelle to safety as soon as possible.

Camille drags Joelle back up the stairs and into her living room. By now Joelle is sobbing uncontrollably.

"Please Camille, please........." Joelle's sobs taper down to an agonizing silence.

Camille guides Joelle over to the sofa. They sit in silence for an eternity before Camille starts to speak.

"Joelle, if you want to give your daughter a chance, this is it. You must let her go." Says Camille. She pulls Joelle, her dearest friend, to her as Joelle buries her head into Camille's shoulder.

"I know, I know." Says Joelle struggling to talk, the

sobs have returned, and they are taking her breath away in uncontrollable gulps.

Camille remembers the first time she met Joelle. She was looking for a seamstress to make her wedding dress. An acquaintance recommended Joelle.

"She's the best, she knows the latest fashions and where to get the finest fabric. Her work is superb, impeccable!"

So, Camille wandered into her shop months before her wedding date and the two became fast friends. They would always end a fitting with a cup of tea and sweets. Joelle would put a record on the turntable to play the latest blues and jazz songs from America. The last record she would play would be Billie Holiday, her favorite singer. Camille and Joelle would sing along, often dancing as well. The tea dates continued well after the wedding. They continued for years, never ending.

And now, here they were. Trying to save Gabrielle's future and most likely her life. What has happened to their world, their beautiful world of tea and lemons, shortbread and petit-fours, girlfriends telling secrets no one else will ever hear. They would sit among the lace and velvet, silk and wool fabrics. The sound of their laughter and singing mingling with the ribbons and trim strewn about the floor.

"Please calm down Joelle, let me explain the plan. Let me explain the escape plan for Gabrielle. This is the secret we must always keep. No one must ever know." Camille says sternly.

XXIV.   Le Bristol

"Le Bristol Hotel is currently under the protection of the United States as per an agreement put forth by Ambassador Bullitt of the United States. Therefore, German officers are currently not allowed to take control of the hotel or stay there. This knowledge comes to me from my husband who has dined in the Ambassador's company at The Ritz Hotel. Of course, all that will change if the Americans enter the war, but for now the Hotel cannot be occupied by any German soldiers or officers." Camille begins to explain to Joelle.

"It was brought to my husband's attention that one Anne Morgan, daughter of the very wealthy J. P. Morgan of America has booked fourteen rooms on the fourth floor of Le Bristol. Like her famous father was, Anne is quite a philanthropist. She is a great friend to the people of France. Anne contributed to the relief efforts here during 'The Great War' and she has returned again to provide much needed aid to our country. At first, it was thought these rooms were being held for her staff and herself. My husband has been secretly informed that they are being reserved to assist Jews hoping to get out of Paris and to America." Camille continues. Joelle is speechless, and the first glimmer of hope has appeared on her weary face. Camille can almost see her beautiful smile hidden beneath the veil of worry.

"Pierre then approached Miss Morgan as she dined with a friend at The Ritz Hotel. He told her about Gabrielle, as I informed him of your wish to get her to safety now. She listened to Pierre thoughtfully. She promised to get back to him. The next week he received a note from her as he dined at The Ritz again. A waiter discretely dropped it at his table as he passed by. It simply said. '*Apporter Gabrielle. 5 novembre à minuit.*'

"Thank you Camille! Thank you my dearest friend." Says Joelle.

"You have done the right thing Joelle. I will keep you updated. I will let you know as soon as I get a letter from her. I promise. Also, you must keep your guard up. You must trust no one. There is danger right on your street. I am going to get you out of Paris, either to join Gabrielle or to send you south to the unoccupied zone where it is safer. Oh, and by the way, get a new hairdresser. Claudette is keeping company with a German officer. She never was a great stylist anyway. Look at her scruffy hair! Mon Dieu!" Camille says with a giggle trying to inject some humor to lighten up the unbearable sadness Joelle is feeling. But the humor falls flat, nothing will cheer Joelle until she is reunited with Gabrielle and Philip.

As Camille leaves she glances across the street at the salon. She notices the German officer and Claudette have moved their tête-à-tête inside and they are sharing a glass of wine. Claudette observes Camille's disapproving look and reaches for the window sash and pulls the shade down. Has the whole world gone mad, Camille wonders?

XXV.   Room 422

Gabrielle sits on her twin bed. It is her first morning she has ever spent without her mother. By the time she arrived at Le Bristol and got settled into a room it was 1:30 in the morning. After a cup of hot chocolate and a warm croissant she is shown to her bed and given a beautiful lace and cotton night-dress to sleep in. Frightened and overwhelmed with sadness, she did not sleep a wink.

Besides Gabrielle, the room is also occupied by a family. A mother, father and three girls. She notices a girl who appears to be the same age as her, around fifteen years old. The young girl smiles at Gabrielle and Gabrielle smiles back. The girl walks over and sits next to Gabrielle.

"What is your name." she asks. "Gabrielle, what is yours?" Gabrielle asks. "Elise." She replies. "We are going to America." Elise explains.

"I am too. I am going to Brooklyn, New York. My Mama and Papa will follow when my Papa comes home from the war. My Mama is waiting for him and then they will join me." Says Gabrielle in a matter-of-fact way, knowing deep inside that it may not play out as she hopes. She pushes any doubt of a family reunion out of her thoughts. She must think positively. She must will it to be true….. that she will see her Mama and Papa again soon.

The two sit there and talk about America and leaving home. Gabrielle is thankful to have a new friend to talk to. It is a distraction from the fear and sadness she is feeling.

As they sit there the door to the suite suddenly opens. A very tall and striking older woman wearing the most beautiful dress and exquisite hat walks in. She looks around the room and smiles. Her vibrancy fills the room. She is bigger than life. Gabrielle stares at her in awe.

"That's Miss Morgan! She's the American helping us. She is wonderful! And funny too! She always makes us laugh…..She speaks perfect French, just like us! Wait until you hear her speak! You will be amazed!" Says Elise.

Anne Morgan makes her way around the room, greeting everyone. She comes to Gabrielle and kneels in front of her. She takes both of Gabrielle's hands in hers and looks into her eyes. Miss Morgan eyes are warm and calming. Gabrielle suddenly feels at ease in the company of this incredible woman.

"You must be Gabrielle! What a brave girl you are!" she says as she tightens her hold on Gabrielle's hands. Gabrielle notices Miss Morgan's French is impeccable as Elise mentioned.

"Soon you will be in America! You will be there before you know it! Ah, I have a book for you!" she says and hands Gabrielle 'The Count of Monte Cristo' by Alexandre Dumas. "It's my favorite adventure." She adds as she leans in and kisses Gabrielle on both cheeks. And then she is gone. Her expensive French perfume lingers in the room.

Gabrielle sits on her bed looking at her beautiful gift.

The book is bound in deep red leather with gold edges on each page. A beautiful illustration of 'The Count' graces the front cover. Gabrielle opens the book. She sees that Miss Morgan has written something inside. It reads.....

Dear Gabrielle,

Life is an adventure. You are about to embark on the biggest adventure of your life. I promise you that all the sadness you feel at this moment will be replaced by joy one day soon. You will have a full and wonderful life in America.'

Yours—Anne Morgan, November 1940.

Gabrielle holds the book to her chest. She vows to keep the book safe with her for the rest of her life. She feels such deep gratitude toward Miss Morgan. This woman, a stranger, so filled with compassion for others she is risking her own safety.......perhaps even her life to save others. She turns the page, and she begins to read. She slowly drifts to sleep.

XXVI.   Miss Morgan's Last Visit

G abrielle spends one full week at Le Bristol. She spends
her time reading and chatting with Elise about all of
their hopes and dreams. They become good friends and
promise to stay in touch when they reach America.

On the seventh day of her stay, Miss Morgan enters
the room. This time she is serious, her lightheartedness
has been put aside.

"Please listen carefully. It is time to pack up all of your
belongings. Tonight, at midnight you will be leaving
Le Bristol to make the journey to Lisbon, Portugal and
then on to America. There will be a car provided for your
journey to Lisbon. The journey will take three days. You
will be driving straight through, only stopping for petrol.
We will provide a basket of food, enough to make the
entire journey to Lisbon. When you reach Lisbon, you
will be staying at a small villa until an aeroplane is safely
secured for your journey to New York City. The car
will be stopped at the border checkpoint between France
and Spain. You must show them the visa's and papers I
have provided for you and say nothing. Then you will
be stopped again when you reach Portugal. Everything
is in proper order, so you should reach Lisbon without
any interruption in your journey." Miss Morgan explains
knowing full well they are in constant danger.

Anne Morgan realizes that it will only cause more anxiety if they are provided with the reality of the danger they are being face with. She can tell by the expressions on their faces that they are fully aware of their precarious predicament. It is a life-or-death journey they are embarking on. It could go either way.

Miss Morgan makes her way around the room, wishing all of them a safe journey. Again, she kneels in front of Gabrielle and takes Gabrielle's hands in hers. "Soon you will be safe, my '*courageuse juene femme*" Miss Morgan says.

"Godspeed!" Miss Morgan says as she leaves them. They are now in the hands of destiny and fate. She has taken them as far as she can, hoping that these six will make it safely to America as the others before them have. Thus far Anne Morgan's plan to relocate refugees from Paris to America via Le Bristol Hotel has been successful. They have all arrived safely in America.

As Anne Morgan walks the long, lush hall, lit by the crystal-jeweled sconces that lead to her room, tears once again fall unbridled down her cheeks. She wonders if it will ever end, a world filled with so much hatred. A world that rejects peace and empathy in favor of war and destruction.

XXVII.   The Journey

At midnight there is a soft knock at the door. Elise's father slowly opens the door. There is a man standing there holding a lantern. "It is time." He says.

The six of them pick up their small suitcases and move toward the door. Gabrielle stays close to Elise. Elise grabs Gabrielle's hand. They are both shaking with fear. Gabrielle tries to hold back the tears. She thinks of her mother and leaving her behind. It is all too much. She most push all the feelings aside for now. She thinks of Miss Morgan, and she wills herself to act brave.

They are led to a staircase that leads to the first floor. From there they are led through the kitchen to a door at the back of Le Bristol. It leads to a narrow alley. A black car is parked there, and they get in. Elise's father is handed the key. He is carrying a map that he has been studying for the past week. It will take them on the safest and fastest route. They drive slowly through the empty Parisian streets. They have to maneuver and make some quick turns to avoid being spotted. The map they are given provides a studied route that helps them avoid the Nazi soldiers throughout of the city. They are traveling through the dark unlit countryside of France, on their way south to Spain and then to Portugal.

The journey takes three days as Miss Morgan pre-
dicted. They drive straight through, stopping only for a
quick meal and rest. It seems like a dream; they make the
journey safely all the way to Lisbon. The false papers, provided by Ann Morgan, deliver them to their destination
without any difficulty. They are a non-Jewish Parisian
family according to their falsified papers. It is November
of 1940 and immigrating out of France is still possible for
the fortunate few. But that will soon change for the Parisians who have chosen to stay behind.

Gabrielle is sleeping when the car pulls up to a beautiful villa on the outskirts of Lisbon. Elise gently touches
her shoulder to wake her. It is the middle of the night.
Elise's father parks the car, and they walk up the cobble
driveway to the front door. The door is opened by a
lovely middle-aged woman.

"Welcome to my home, my name is Cassandra." She
says with a warm smile. She then stands aside and motions
them in.

They enter a large foyer in silent relief. The room
is painted in a cream color as is the furniture. The large
table in the middle of the room holds an enormous vase
filled with dozens of long stem white roses. The floor is a
shiny checkerboard of black and white marble. A winding staircase leading to the second floor is covered with a
white rose patterned carpet. The railing is black wrought
iron, decorated with wrought iron roses and fleur-de-lis.
Gabrielle gazes around the beautiful foyer, she has never
seen a home so majestic.

The woman guides them into a dining room dimly

lit by an enormous blue crystal chandelier. The art deco sideboard is filled with sandwiches and pastry.

"Please help yourself, you must be ravenous." She then offers the adults a glass of wine and the young ones of cup of hot chocolate and fresh whipped cream. Hot chocolate has never tasted so good to Gabrielle.

Gabrielle and the three girls are then taken upstairs to two bedrooms. Elise and Gabrielle stay together in one of them. They jump onto the high, canopied bed. Elise lets out a giggle and Gabrielle allows herself to join in. They change into their nightdresses and start to explore the room.

It is decorated completely in red velvet. An intricately carved mahogany bureau is adorned with perfumes, a vase of red roses and a silver filigree frame holding a photograph. Gabrielle notices the photograph is of Cassandra holding hands with a little girl. Cassandra is much younger in the photograph. It must be her and her daughter, many years ago. Her daughter would be older now. Perhaps she has moved away. This must have been her bedroom, Gabrielle imagines.

Gabrielle thinks of her mother, and she remembers the photograph taken on the Seine her mother tucked into her suitcase. She hurries over and opens her bag to retrieve it, it is wrapped in her mother's silk scarf. She holds the scarf against her face, she can smell the scent of her mother's lingering perfume. She places the photograph on the nightstand next to the bed. She falls asleep comforted by the photograph and scarf. She dreams she is searching for her mother; she is just around every corner.

Gabrielle cannot reach her as hard as she tries. She can only hear her mother's voice calling to her. "Gabrielle! Gabrielle, come to Mama s'il vous plaît!"

They spend three days at the villa. Again, they leave in the middle of the night and make their way to an airstrip. They board a plane. Gabrielle and Elise sit side by side. This time Gabrielle reaches for Elise's hand. Fear and sadness mix with the excitement of the journey.

After a few minutes the plane takes flight and they are off, leaving a continent ravaged by war behind them. Gabrielle wonders if she will ever return, she wonders if she will ever see her mother or father again. Tears fall as the plane ascends into the clouds.

XXVIII.   December 1940

Joelle has been without her daughter for over a month. Consumed with sadness, she is determined to get her family back together. She awaits news of Gabrielle and Philip. When Philip returns, she is hoping to immigrate to America to join Gabrielle.

Her dress shop is now completely closed. She does a small amount of dress making in her apartment. With Camille's help, she lugged her best sewing machine up the stairs and into her living room so she could continue to work undetected by the Gestapo.

Camille visits Joelle every day. Each day Joelle is hoping that Camille will show up with a letter in hand from Gabrielle. They sit and have tea every afternoon. Sometime Camille is able to bring the most coveted of the rationed items to Joelle. These include lemons, eggs, flour, butter, cheeses, and bread.

One afternoon she hears a knock on the door, and she opens it. Camille is standing before her carrying a bottle of Perrier-Jouët champagne and a smile on her face. Joelle wonders how she got her hands on such highly sought-after item.

"Sit with me and let's have champagne instead of tea today." Camille says.

Joelle goes to her china cabinet and retrieves two crystal flutes.

Camille pops the cork, and it hits the ceiling. She then reaches in her pocket and takes out a letter. She hands it to Joelle.

Joelle sees the postage stamp first 'Air Mail, United States of America,' Her eyes are so filled with tears she can hardly see the neat and beautiful penmanship of her daughter. Joelle is so overwhelmed she starts to fall to the floor. But Camille steps in to catch her, and then they both fall together. They fall in a loving heap filled with tears of joy for Gabrielle. Their Gabrielle has made it! Soon the tears are replaced with the sound of their laughter as they disentangle and manage to get back on their feet.

Joelle opens the letter slowly and gently, as not to tear any part of it. It is as if she is holding her daughter in her hands. Before she reads it she brings the letter to touch her face and she inhales deeply. Perhaps the scent of her daughter has traveled across the Atlantic Ocean with the letter and still lingers on the page. And yes, there it is! The familiar scent of her daughter. The scent only a mother would recognize.

Dear Mama,

I have made it safely to America! It took only six days! We drove straight through to Lisbon. From Lisbon we took an aeroplane to New York! It was quite frightening and exciting at the same time, if that is possible!

I met Miss Anne Morgan at Le Bristol. She is such a kind and lovely lady! She gave me a book by Alexandre Dumas, 'The Count of Monte Cristo'! I have read it twice! I keep it on my nightstand with the photograph of me, you and Papa on the Seine.

I met a girl named Elise at Le Bristol. I made the journey with her and her family. When we arrived in Lisbon, we stayed in the most extravagant villa! It was high on a hill and surrounded by beautiful gardens and lemon trees.

When we finally arrived in New York Elise's Papa helped me find my way to cousin Samuel and Martine's home in Brooklyn. What a strange and wonderful place New York is! There are all kinds of people living in Brooklyn from all different parts of the world. Samuel's daughter Chloe has shown me most of the neighborhood. The smells are strange, not like Paris. The streets are crowded with outdoor markets and they smell spicy and foreign to me. Yet, I suppose I will get used to it. Cousin Samuel and Martine have been wonderful. I share a bedroom with Chloe and sometimes we stay up late into the night talking. She loves to hear about Paris.

I miss you so much Mama! Has Papa returned? I miss him so! Is he safe? When will you and Papa be joining me in America? Please write back as soon as you can!

Je t'aime! Je t'aime! Je t'aime!

—Your Gabrielle

When Joelle is done reading the letter, Camille pours them both a full flute of champagne. The bubbles escape over the rim and run down the sides of each glass.

They raise their glasses for a toast. "A notre ange Gabrielle!" Camille says. "A notre ange Gabrielle!" Joelle repeats.

"I will be back tomorrow to pick up your letter in response to Gabrielle's! I know you! You will be up all night writing your reply!" Camille says while she leans in to kiss Joelle on both cheeks. "Sleep well mon cher, your angel is safe!" she adds and then she is gone.

The following day Camille returns early in the morning to visit Joelle and retrieve the letter she has written to Gabrielle. She knocks softly and Joelle does not answer. She begins to knock harder and realizes the door is not fully shut. Camille walks slowly into Joelle's apartment.

"Joelle! Joelle!" Camille says as she starts to panic. "Joelle!" she repeats.

Camille slowly makes her way through the apartment. When she gets to Joelle's bedroom she notices clothes strewn around the room. Her closet is half empty. Camille realizes that Joelle has hastily packed some belongings and left.

"Dear God!" Camille says out loud as she slowly sits on Joelle's bed. What has happened to my dear friend? She sits there for a while trying to imagine what has transpired. Her mind races as she ponders different scenario's. Then she gets up and leaves the apartment. She must find out what has become of Joelle.

When Camille opens the downstairs door and walks

outside, she notices Claudette staring at her from her salon across the street. Camille crosses the street in haste to speak to her.

"Do you know what has happened to Joelle? Have you seen her?" Camille asks.

"Who cares?" Claudette replies.

Camille responds with a heavy slap across Claudette's smug face, leaving her stunned and speechless.

"Shame on you, Claudette! Shame on you! You are a traitor to your own people and consorting with the enemy! Did you forget you are a Parisian? Did you forget you are married, and your husband is a prisoner of war? How can you live with yourself?" Camille says as she walks away in disgust, leaving Claudette standing there with a smarting red imprint of a hand on her left cheek.

'What has happened to my city, my beautiful city?', Camille wonders as she vows to find her dear friend Joelle.

XXIX. Jaime in London

Jaime settles into his small flat in the Chelsea section of London, overlooking the Thames. It is a tiny efficiency; the bed, stove, sink and ice box are in the same room. There is a small Formica topped table with two chairs. The only separate room is the bathroom. The bed is a twin, pushed up against the wall. There is one window in the room. He moves the dusty curtain to look out. His view consists of a narrow alleyway and a window directly across from him. If he opened the window, he could reach and touch his neighbor's window. He quickly shuts the curtain.

A message has been slipped under his door informing him where and when he is to meet the agent working for the British Security Service, MI5 division.

The M15 will implement the successful 'double-cross system' during WWII, which includes giving false information to enemy spies. The enemy spies will pass on this false information to the German secret service known as Abwehr. M15 is also successful in 'turning' captured German spies. They will agree to serve the British cause to avoid being executed.

The next day Jaime heads out to meet his connection from the British Intelligence agency. He is shocked and saddened by the condition of London. There are blocks and blocks of bombed out buildings, the city is in ruins. The devastation is reflected on the faces of the people he passes in the street on his way to meet his contact. They are tired and toughened. They walk with rigid shoulders defiant in the face of death. They are rebuilding their beloved city after the horrific damage incurred during the Blitz of London, when the Germans consistently bombed the city into ruins.

The Germans abandon their sights on an invasion of Great Britain temporarily to turn their sights on Russia. A decision that will come back to haunt Hitler and his army. Russia will prove to be a mighty force. The Brits and allies realize it is now or never to defeat the enemy, or they will return with a vengeance.

The British have been living under the constant fear of attack. Jaime is now facing the realization that he is in the midst of this persistent threat also. The realization of the danger he is now facing hits him all at once and he leans against the crumbling wall of a bombed-out building to catch his breath. He reaches in his pocket to grab the north star charm. It comforts him for a brief moment, and he thinks of Gia. He manages a smile, even as his heart pounds with fear. But the smile is short lived.

His thoughts turn dark as he is brought back to the task at hand. He knows the enemy lies right in this city. He knows that Nazi sympathizers and spies have set up camp here and are working diligently to inform German Intelligence of every move the allies are making.

Jaime makes his way through the rubble of bricks, dust and destroyed structures to meet with Jonathan Briggs, his contact from MI5. It's time to outsmart the Nazi bastards and beat them at their own game. They meet at a small pub called "The Queen's Revenge", aptly named Jaime concludes with a smile. The pub has miraculously made it through the bombed-out city block it inhabits without a single dent.

Jaime opens an old worn, heavily carved wooden door. As he enters, he ducks under the low doorway obviously built in a time when men and women had smaller frames.

Inside the doorway he notices a small bronze plaque. *'Erected in the year of our Lord 1583. Frequently visited by Queen Elizabeth'.*

The low ceiling with ancient, blackened beams and white stucco walls and ceiling are a telling signs of its age. It is built in the Tudor style. 'My god', Jaime thinks… ….a pub that existed during the reign of Queen Elizabeth. Hallowed ground.

'What would Elizabeth do in these trying times? The Queen who would orchestrate the defeat of the entire Spanish Armada.' Jaime ponders with a wry smile.

He walks slowly and deeper into the room allowing his eyes to adjust to the darkness. A young man at the bar nods to him and waves him over. To others, it appears that the two are old friends meeting for a drink.

The bar is a highly polished dark mahogany. The bar fits eight faded green leather topped barstools. The shelves in the back of the bar are sparsely stocked with various half empty bottles of liquor and wine. In times of peace, the shelves would be full and brimming with a wide variety of libations.

A tiny oil painting of Queen Elizabeth with her flaming red hair and famous Elizabethan collar rests in between the bottles. Its ancient frame is intricately carved. The painting needs a good dusting and restoration. Jaime can surmise immediately that the painting is almost as old as the pub. It was most likely painted during the Queen's lifetime.

The young man extends his hand to shake Jaime's. "Hello, I'm Jon. Tea, wine or beer is about all they have here bloke. Care for a pint?" He says in a cheerful 'don't give a damn' sort of way.

"Yes, I'll take a pint." Jaime replies as he takes a seat next to Jon. The barmaid is an older woman with a friendly face. She brings them their beer and a plate of tiny egg salad sandwiches. The bread is slightly stale, but they gobble them up. They are delicious.

Jon speaks surprisingly open in front of the barmaid, and he recognizes the concern in Jaime's eyes. "Clara is one of us, this neighborhood seems to be swarming with Nazi sympathizers. She's already overheard five conversations between Nazi spies, and they've been rounded up after they are followed a good distance from the pub. This ensures the others will keep coming here for her famous egg salad sandwiches."

"We now refer to them as 'Clara's 'eiersalat-fuckers', because apparently the sandwiches appeal to the Nazi bastards." Jon explains as they all break into laughter.

Jaime marvels at the fact that laughter still exists in London, yet he knows it is part of what keeps these war-trodden people going. The Brits never lose their resiliency or their sense of humor when times get tough.

Jon and Jaime get down to the business at hand.

"Within the next couple of days, you will be receiving a package that will explain your assignment. The drop off will be made at the pub on the corner next to your flat, 'The Sword and Crown'. You must go there every day at noon until the drop is made. Be sure to sit at one of the tables in the back of the pub." Jon explains.

Jaime is not informed from whom the package will arrive, he is not privy to that information.

He is informed that from this point forward he is not allowed to have any interaction with anyone but Jonathan. Not even a letter home to Gia or his family. For the next several weeks he is on his own, he must remain under the radar.

Jaime returns to his dismal flat and falls into a much-needed sleep, he dreams of Gia standing at a train station wearing a white summer dress. She is smiling and waving….. as his train pulls away. Her dress swirls in the wake of the train. She calls out to him, but her voice is muted by the roar of the train.

He awakes with a start. He hears voices in the hall. Whispers. He lies still and breaks into a cold sweat. He can no longer trust the strangers he meets. According to Jonathan, German sympathizers and spies are lurking everywhere in London. He is far from home and so close to the enemy he can feel their dark presence. Gia does not show up in his next dream. Instead, his dreams of Gia are replaced with German soldiers. They wear smoky gray uniforms and red swastika armbands. Stomping jackboots.

On Jaime's fourth visit to the designated meeting

place near his flat, a young woman wearing a drab grey coat and a red plaid scarf enters the pub. She sees Jaime and sits at the table next to him. She stares straight ahead, avoiding further eye contact. He sees that she is carrying a small brown package. She places it on the floor.

She orders a cup of tea and a sandwich. She eats in silence and walks out, leaving the package on the floor. Jaime quickly scoops up the package and saunters out of the pub carrying the most important and dangerous envelope he will ever take possession of.

Jaime returns to his flat and props up the old feather pillows on the bed. He lies down, opens the package and begins to read.

XXX. The Hope

J aime's mission is to visit a pub called 'The Hope.' It is located next to a factory located in East London. The factory is known to be a cover for harboring Nazi sympathizers and spies. Although the British government could essentially shut the factory down, they realize that by letting it operate as usual, the British Intelligence Agencies can utilize these active spies as messengers of false information. They can also infiltrate the factory with some of the German spies who have been caught and turned by British Intelligence. Keep your enemy close is the plan.

The pub is frequented by an infamous Nazi spy named Greta Wagner who works at the factory during the day. The package describes her as a Berliner who has immigrated to London to work at the German factory. She is well educated and ruthless in her ambition to aid the Nazi's in a victory over the allies. Her position at the factory is a cover while she resides in London.

Jaime's mission is to befriend her, convince her he is also a Nazi sympathizer and provide her with the false information that the Allies will be invading Pas-de-Calais and Norway. The Allies need to spread the German army thin along the coasts of France. They need to ensure that the Normandy beaches do not have the maximum number of German troops congregated at the shores they are planning to land on.

The false locations for the impending invasion are being rumored by all the double-cross agents in hopes it will reach German Intelligence in Berlin. Jaime will attempt to convince Greta that he has gathered this information by intercepting British Intelligence radio transmissions. Because he is so familiar with the inner workings of the monitoring station at Chopmist Hill, he should be able to persuade her and any of her co-conspirators that he is providing them with truthful information.

His other task is to find out how Greta is transmitting messages and where the radio equipment is hidden. The spies working for the Nazi's have come in with self-contained suitcases outfitted with radio transmitters. Jonathan, from MI5 is convinced Greta has an accomplice at the factory who is transmitting the messages back to the Abwehr in Berlin.

Jaime will visit the pub three times before he is absolutely positive he has identified Greta from the photograph that was supplied in the package he received. He overhears another woman calling out her name as she walks in the door. Greta immediately strides toward the table where the woman is seated with a man. Jaime lingers by their table to eavesdrop on their conversation. The three speak to each other in German.

He is surprised by her appearance; she is absolutely stunning. The photograph in the package has clearly failed to convey her beauty. She is tall and lean with a hauntingly beautiful face. She is dressed smartly, wearing a tight black skirt and a cream silk blouse. Her hair is long and dark, swept up in a French twist. Her eyes are steel blue. She has accented them with dark coal liner. Her lips are full and painted red.

He tries to act casual, but he admits to himself that it is a struggle to keep his eyes off of her. In his opinion, she is perfectly poised to extract any information she needs from anyone she wants. She is undeniably captivating, a perfect disguise for her troubling mission.

He notices she is staring at him, so he takes the opportunity to approach her table. The three regard Jaime with interest and wariness as he stands over the table. He introduces himself as Gustav Winter. He lays on his thickest Berlin accent as he speaks. He thinks of his father as he hears his own voice mimicking him perfectly. But Jaime has added a bit of coldness to his voice that his father, thankfully, lacks.

Greta's relief in hearing his German accent is evident in her body language. She suddenly relaxes. She gracefully extends her hand for him to kiss. "Greta Wagner, it is a pleasure to meet you." she says as she eyes him from head to foot. He notices her long slender fingers and her beautifully sculpted hands. Her fingernails are painted blood red to match her lips. He immediately makes a mental note that these are not the hands of a factory worker. No callouses or broken nails for this woman, her hands are smooth and supple. Of course, he already knows that. She has been living a pampered life, while others are suffering. She must be spending her days in the office of a high-ranking Nazi official; she is a spy hiding in plain sight at the factory and here at the pub. Her arrogance has led her to believe she is untouchable.

Her demeanor is quite welcoming. She slides further into the booth allowing him the opportunity to move seamlessly into the offered space. He can see that she is so incredibly confidant that no man would ever refuse the invite she offers. Her arrogance has also led her to believe she is irresistible.

He sits next to her, facing the man and woman. There is no turning back now, he thinks. Full speed ahead for this novice spy, he thinks as his heart pounds so hard he fears they may be able to hear it.

Introductions are offered from across the table. "Wilhelm Lang, nice to meet you" the man says as he rises and leans in to shake Jaime's hand. Jaime notices his shifty eyes and his overly agitated demeanor. His distrust toward Jaime is perceptible in his behavior. It is also evident that Wilhelm is a loose cannon ready to explode, Jaime notes. Jaime tries to remain nonchalant, and he forces a smile to remain on his face.

"Ida Wolf" the woman extends her hand for Jaime to kiss. All speak English in heavy German accents. The conversation is light and is centralized around safe subjects. Eventually they all start to speak in German, leaving the English language behind. Jaime notices that Greta dominates the conversation, and the others seem to look to her for approval. She is in control and Jaime can see the hierarchy of the group puts her on the top.

After some time, Greta leans over to Ida and whispers

something in her ear. Ida smiles and nudges Wilhelm. Ida and Wilhelm stand and make convoluted excuses and leave the pub. Clearly Greta has orchestrated their hasty departure.

Jaime suddenly feels ill at ease sitting alone with her and it's a strain to seem nonchalant. Yet, he realizes that this is his chance to get her talking. He needs to create intimacy between the two of them, so she will begin to trust him. He also has to keep it light and let her lead the conversation.

He is optimistic the information he needs to extract from her will come effortless if he is convincing enough. He is also hopeful she will believe the false information he will be offering her regarding the invasion.

With the others gone, Jaime can take in more of Greta visually. Her outfit is definitely a luxury in London given it is wartime. She wears the finest wool skirt and silk blouse. She has placed an expensive pair of kid gloves on the table. They match her blouse perfectly. She wears dark red suede pumps, matching the color of her lips and nails. He notices she is wearing nylons, a clear give away of her stature. No 'drawn in' lines are traveling up the back of her flawless legs. Only the real deal will do for this 'schöne frau'.

She tilts her head to the side, "Do you have a wife….. or lady friend?" she asks.

"No, not at the moment" he replies while thinking of Gia. He feels a pang of guilt having to lie.

"Shame." she says. "Or maybe not such a shame." she adds with a sheepish giggle. He returns her giggle with a hearty laugh, and it sounds forced. He realizes he needs to play it cool. He must act like he is thoroughly enjoying their playful banter.

"What is your Nachbarschaft?" she asks.

"Pardon"? he asks.

"In Berlin? Your neighborhood?" she asks again.

"Oh, right. Charlottenburg." he replies. God, he thinks. Get on your game. Of course, she will be bringing up Berlin. Commonalities. He feels sweat starting to form on his brow.

"Yours?" he asks.

"Friedrichshain." She replies. Thank god, he thinks. If they were from the same neighborhood, she surely would be asking him what his favorite 'Kneipe' is next. To which, he would have no reply.

The conversation remains light throughout the evening. He can see she is interested in him, so he asks her out for the following Friday night, and they part ways. They agree to meet back at 'The Hope' and then walk to a nearby restaurant. As he leaves the pub, his legs almost give way they are so shaky. But he is confidant she has no idea what his true motive is.

When he returns to his flat, he falls on the bed and sleeps in his clothes he is so emotionally drained. Again, his dreams are troubling and filled with Nazi spies and enemy soldiers.

XXXI. The Second Date

The following Friday, Jaime and Greta meet at 'The Hope', as planned.

Greta has arrived early to share a drink with her two fellow German friends. But of course, these acquaintances are more than just friends. Jaime concurs that they are also spies working for the Nazi's.

"There's something not right about that Gustav Winter, I'm telling you!" Wilhelm says to Greta in a hushed tone filled with anger. "He's a god damn American. I'm sure of it! I can tell by his swagger! He struts around like a cowboy in some corny wild-west film! His accent is off, has some sort of twang to it. I don't trust the son-of-a-bitch!" he adds.

"Don't be an ass!" Greta replies in a hushed angry tone. "I am a Berliner and I know a Berliner when I see one and hear one. There's not a trace of American in that man. Now shut your mouth and calm down, he's standing at the door!" Greta warns and then quickly replaces a frown with an engaging smile.

'What an actress', Jaime thinks. It is clear they take their orders from her; Jaime observes once again. She is the one in command. Wilhelm obeys and forces a smile to form on his hardened face. But the smile arrives a bit too late.

Jaime has already noticed the tension at the table from the pub door as he enters. He wonders if he is the subject of the hostile exchange between Greta and Wilhelm. Most likely, he surmises. He lingers at the door slightly giving them time to calm down. He wants them to believe he has just walked in and has missed their obvious disagreement.

"Gustav!" he hears Greta's musical voice from across the pub. "Over here!" she adds. He strides over with a big smile on his face. He acts seemingly oblivious to their stifled discord. He reaches for her hand and kisses it, giving her an over exaggerated bow. She giggles in return, clearly captivated by him.

"Hello Wilhelm and Ida! I hope you won't be too disappointed! I'm afraid I will be stealing your lovely friend Greta away for the evening! Perhaps we can find somewhere decent to dine in this god-forsaken city!" Jaime says.

He is hoping they don't ask him to stay and have a drink. He needs to get Greta alone and convince her he is trustworthy and on her side without blowing his cover. He needs to move the plan along, so he can wrap the mission up and get home.

Jaime quickly grabs Greta's manicured hand and lifts her from her seat, preventing any interference from Wilhelm and Ida. She leans briefly against him to find her balance. Jaime is slightly shaken by the realization that he enjoys the brief contact with her. He quickly puts himself in check. She is a Nazi spy, and he has no business feeling anything resembling attraction or fondness for her in any way, he is in love after all.

Jaime duly notes the clear dislike in Wilhelm's eyes as

they part ways for the night. His cold gaze hits Jaime like a fist to the gut. In addition to Wilhelm's dislike, Jaime can see the slight hint of doubt in his cold, calculating eyes. Fear takes hold of Jaime, but he pushes it down deep inside him where it will have to remain for the duration of his stay in London. Jaime is now starting to suspect Wilhelm may be the spy sending the messages back to his homeland. His intuition is guiding his suspicions.

Jaime and Greta walk down the street to a quiet restaurant called 'The Victoria'. They settle into a quiet booth in the corner. He can see she has taken her time getting ready for their date. She is perfect. Yet he must remind himself that her beauty only runs skin deep. Jaime must also keep in mind Greta's ambition to destroy everything dear to him. He cannot wait to get the task over and get home. He misses Gia the most at this very moment.

Jaime has been informed by Jonathan that Greta's influence is far reaching. All of the information she gathers goes straight to the top. They call her 'Wunderschönes Juwel', (Beautiful Gem).

They order from a very limited and rationed menu. It is some sort of canned meat and potatoes seasoned with dried herbs and makes for a very bland Shephard's Pie. It is the special of the night. They order brandy, which has obviously been watered down, yet it helps calm Jaime's nerves somewhat.

The conversation starts lightly…..they talk about Berlin and their current home of London. They discuss what it is like to be a German living in Great Britain. There is an obvious dislike and distrust of all Germans residing on English soil. They discuss the unsettled direction of the war and what the outcome may be. As typical of Nazi sympathizers, they unabashedly believe they will prevail and conquer anyone standing in their way. Jaime has a significant inner struggle as he expresses his loyalty and pride for the 'Vaterland'.

Eventually, the conversation turns serious.

"What exactly are you doing here?" she asks as she looks directly into his eyes. Her eyes are cold and flat of emotion. Here is the moment, he thinks. Play it cool.

"I'm here for the exact same reason as you are, and you know it." Jaime replies, sternly and vaguely, not giving her any more of an explanation. He knows he is bluffing his way through this exchange. His eyes are cold and like hers, devoid of any emotion. Christ, he thinks. I'm actually good at this. So this is how it's done. He finds that he is quite the actor, and it surprises and scares him at the same time. He is amazed by his coldness but realizes that this is what transpires in the face of danger. This is what he must do to survive this encounter and get the job done successfully so he can get home alive.

There is silence between the two of them for a while. Suddenly the drama of the situation hits Jaime. It seems somewhat comedic to him, as if the two of them are starring in a melodramatic film. He finds he is actually suppressing a laugh. He disguises it with a cough. He contributes his sudden urge to laugh to the tension he is feeling brought on by the circumstances. 'Gather yourself together and put yourself in check' he thinks.

The conversation finally starts up again. He is able to

convince her that he has been intercepting radio transmissions sent by British Intelligence. She prods him for more information. He assures her of his intelligence gathering expertise.

His experience at Chopmist Hill and his command of a perfect Berlin accent allows him to pull off the ruse.

She is warmed by the brandy she sips and the company she keeps. She leans in to kiss him and inhales the information he supplies her as if drawing on a rare rationed cigarette. His task is almost complete, by midnight the highest-ranking Gestapo officers will be raising their glasses of looted vintage wine to toast a lovingly placed British lie.

He easily convinces her to stay a little longer and share another drink. He walks up to the bar and leans in to whisper to the bartender.

"Anything stronger or not watered down behind there my friend?" Jaime says.

The bartender smiles and nods, realizing Jaime is an American, and reaches deep under the bar.

"This bottle is reserved especially for Winston Churchill or a wayward visiting Yank." The bartender says in a whisper just for the two of them to hear. He pulls up a bottle of Johnny Walker Blue and places it on the bar.

"Here you go, my friend from across the pond." He says as he pours it into two ancient snifter glasses. "Enjoy and soldier on, as they say!" He adds with a smile mixed with admiration and mutual comradery.

Jaime heads back to the table carrying the two glasses with one hand, wearing a smug smile on his face. He gently places the two glasses on the table. They clink glasses to toast a German victory. Jaime secretly dedicates his toast to Winston Churchill. They sip in silence for a while, both enjoying a rare taste of perfection. The scotch warms them, relaxes them.

Jaime patiently waits for the delicious nectar to take full effect on Greta. He can see Greta's eyes begin to look sleepy and seductive at the same time. He leans in to ask the last question he will ever ask her. He must know for sure who is sending the transmissions to Abwehr. She replies with the answer he has known all along. "Wilhelm." She says, a slight slur affects her speech.

Jaime and Greta linger outside of 'The Victoria.' He can tell she is taken with him. She looks into his eyes. He tries to avoid returning her gaze, but he cannot keep from glancing back into her eyes. He is struck again by her beauty.

For a brief moment he is tempted to wrap his arms around her waist and pull her against him and kiss her. But he resists and instead he stares directly into her beautiful eyes. ….asking without speaking. Why?

But she does not offer him an answer and the spell is broken. He backs away and releases her from his captive heart for good. His mission is almost complete. He has completed step one. Relief and sadness hit him at the same time.

She asks if they might meet again. He says 'yes' knowing he will never see her again. He kisses her lightly on the cheek and he watches her walk away. He feels sorrow for her. He knows that her life will be cut short for being on the wrong side of history, for being on the wrong side of what is just and true. He wonders how she could be so terribly wrong.

XXXII.   The Black Swan

Jaime makes his way back to his flat. He walks slowly, lost in his thoughts. He is relieved his work is almost complete here and soon he will be headed home to Gia. His next step is to inform MI5 that Wilhelm Lang is their man. Wilhelm has been transmitting information he has gathered in London back to the Abwehr since the summer of 1939. That is the day he parachuted from a German fighter plane sent by the Luftwaffe and dangerously touched down on British soil.

Jaime is able to extract a good amount of information from Greta regarding Wilhelm. A ruthless thug, Wilhelm once strangled a man to death outside a bar in Berlin for foolishly approaching and flirting with his girlfriend. To avoid prison Wilhelm's father, a high-ranking Nazi officer, agrees to send him to London to work as a spy for the Fatherland.

Jaime is so caught up in his thoughts as he is walking back to his flat, he doesn't realize that someone is following him. When it becomes apparent someone is close behind him, he flushes with anger at his own stupidity. He remembers Jonathan's first words of advice. Never let your guard down. Never let anyone follow you, you could blow the whole operation, put others in danger and get yourself killed at the same time.

He changes course slightly and starts to walk toward a busier street. He does this for his own protection as well as hoping to find a busy pub to duck into.

He picks up his pace, as does his pursuer. The sound of heels on the cobblestones behind him reminds him of his nightmares. Gray uniforms, goose-stepping Nazi jackboots. It takes everything he has not to break into a run. Keep it even, he thinks……keep it cool. There! Up ahead!…..'The Black Swan'. He sweeps in and dashes to the nearest window.

There he is, Wilhelm Lang! His face is ruddy with anger as he turns on his heels and vanishes down the closest alleyway.

Jaime falls into a seat by the window, nearly knocking over a standing patron on his way.

"Fancy a pint?" the pretty waitress says to him with a big smile. "Yup" he replies. "I fancy a FEW pints as a matter of fact." he adds. He allows himself two pints, which go down much too fast, and then he makes his way back to his flat. This time, he makes sure he is not being followed.

He moves an old bureau in front of his door, as if that would keep a determined murdering Nazi out. He laughs as he falls on the bed, exhausted and feeling the effects of the alcohol. Within a minute he is out cold.

The next day Jaime informs Jonathan that Wilhelm Lang is their man. He is the one transmitting the messages to the Abwehr. He also informs him that he is being followed by Wilhelm and that Wilhelm needs to be scooped up now.

Jonathan agrees that they must act now and apprehend him. But he has one more task for Jaime. He must follow Wilhelm and find out where he is keeping the clandestine radio equipment. He must find the suitcase that has been fitted with the best spy equipment of the time. British Intelligence also wants to get their hands on the 'state of the art' equipment being used by the Nazi's.

It is a dangerous job knowing that Wilhelm's history points to an easily enraged man, a murderer, and a Nazi. A deadly combination.

"Follow him to his flat. The next day, stake out his place until he leaves, get in and grab the equipment. It's portable….look for a leather suitcase. It is so portable he dropped out of a god damn aeroplane carrying it." Jonathan explains. "Just be safe, in and out and you're done. Are you up for it Jaime?" He asks knowing Jaime does not have a choice in the matter.

"Of course" agrees Jaime. "I'm up for the task." he replies. He keeps his disappointment to himself. This was not part of the original plan. He thought he was done and headed home.

He remembers his Mum saying, "Always expect the unexpected!" and it brings a brief smile to his face. But the smile is fleeting. There is no denying the danger he will now be facing.

As he makes his way back to his Chelsea flat, he walks slowly considering his new assignment. He will have to start following Wilhelm and avoid being seen. Wilhelm is a killer in addition to being a Nazi spy, so the stakes are higher. He thinks of Gia, they have had no contact since he left in March. It is mid-May and the invasion of Normandy Beach is less than four weeks away. Jaime finally reaches his flat and falls on the bed. He has a sleepless night thinking of his final task in London.

XXXIII.   Wilhelm

Jaime leaves his apartment and takes a taxi to within a block of 'The Hope' pub. It is 7:30 on a Friday night. Jaime hopes to linger undiscovered outside the pub in the hopes that Wilhelm has shown up for his 'after-work' drink and has stayed to socialize.

He finds the perfect spot across the street in a little bar called 'The Jester's Folly'. It is a dingy little place that someone like Wilhelm would most likely avoid. He sits at the bar with a perfect view of 'The Hope' and orders fish and chips. He washes it down with a pint of beer. Wilhelm does not appear this Friday night, so Jaime heads back to Chelsea and decides to try Saturday night instead.

The following night Jaime retraces his steps. As he rounds the corner he sees Wilhelm heading into 'The Jester's Folly'. He stops short and slowly walks backward into the dark shelter of a deep doorway diagonally across from the bar. Several thoughts cross his mind. Did he see Jaime there last night? Is Wilhelm hoping Jaime will return? Or is he meeting someone there? Jaime can only wait and hope that Wilhelm is not on to him.

Jaime waits for an hour and a half and is just about to give up and find a pub to grab a bite when the door of the bar opens. Wilhelm steps out and Jaime notices he is walking with a slight stagger. "Good." Jaime whispers to himself. This means he has been drinking and will not be on top of his game. Wilhelm has gotten sloppy and he has let his guard down.

Jaime steps out of his hiding place and begins to follow Wilhelm at a safe distance. Jaime and Wilhelm are the only ones on this side of the darkened street. Wilhelm is clearly feeling the effects of the alcohol.

He is singing a German lullaby that Jaime recognizes from his childhood. It is a beautiful song his mother would sing to him to lull him to sleep. *'Guten Abend und gute Nacht!* By Brahms. "Good evening, goodnight. Watched over by angels. In a dream they show you the Christ-child's tree." sings Wilhelm as he stumbles down the street.

The beautiful song his mother so lovingly sang to him at bedtime has taken on an ominous and frightening tone. It sounds harsh and filled with drunken anger coming out of Wilhelm's mouth. The words are slurred, guttural and distorted.

Jaime tries to stay calm and at a safe distance as he follows Wilhelm. As it turns out, Wilhelm lives only three blocks from 'The Hope'. Jaime ducks into another doorway and watches Wilhelm fumble with a key to the front door of a large brick Tudor-style row-house. It houses several small flats. Years ago, the building must have been a beauty. Yet time has not been kind to the stately old building, and it has been left to slowly decay.

Wilhelm walks in and turns to shut the front door. He is so drunk that he does not shut the door completely, the latch does not connect properly and the door slowly creeps opens just a hair. This seems much too easy Jaime thinks as he catches up. He sees Wilhelm ascending the old worn stairs adorned with wrought iron railings. The stairs are carpeted with a runner that is threadbare in the middle from constant use over many years. The building has seen better days, Jaime notes.

Jaime enters the building and slowly ascends the same stairs. The stairs creak slightly, so Jaime tries to tread lightly. When he figures out which apartment Wilhelm is in, his second task will almost be complete. He can return to retrieve the suitcase tomorrow when Wilhelm is not at home and his mission will be done here in London. He will finally be able to head home.

Jaime walks slowly up the winding stairs to the second floor and then he slowly ascends to the third floor. Strange, he cannot see Wilhelm on the stairs leading to the fourth floor as he stares up from the third-floor landing.

He hears something from behind him and spins around. Wilhelm is standing there. Jaime realizes that he is the one who has let his guard down. Wilhelm has followed him, and he is clearly not drunk at all.

He is smiling and says to Jaime. "How did you like the lullaby? Did it remind you of Berlin or America?" Wilhelm says as he lunges at Jaime brandishing a knife he had concealed in his coat pocket.

Jaime tries to grab the knife. When he does he realizes that Wilhelm is incredibly strong. Much stronger than him. Jaime holds his wrist at bay, but the blade is inching closer to him. 'Christ, he thinks. His mind is racing,

flashes of Gia, his parents. Could this be the end.......'
The adrenaline kicks in! Jaime is younger so his stamina is lasting longer than Wilhelm's.

"I am not going to die here and not by you, you no good Nazi son-of-bitch." Jaime says seething and with every breath he can muster. He doesn't even recognize his own voice; it sounds so infuriated.

They struggle for quite a long time and Jaime manages to hold the knife at bay, until Wilhelm manages to nick his cheek. That catapults Jaime's strength into high gear and he pounces on Wilhelm.

They both end up falling intertwined down the stairway to the second floor and smack into a doorway.

The door is promptly opened by a heavy-set woman. She is covered in flour and holding a rolling pin. With a proper good aim, she hits Wilhelm square over the head, knocking him out cold. Blood trickles down his forehead. Jaime quickly jumps to his feet.

"Jesus! Good shot!" Jaime exclaims.

"Damn Nazi got what he deserved. I've had my eye on that bastard for quite a while. Lives in the flat right across from me. Been up to no good since he moved here back in '39. Coming and going with the other Jerry's since the onset of this god-forsaken war. Now how can I help you love? Fancy a tea and biscuit, before we ring the 'bobbies'? My name is Dorothy, by the way. Pardon my disarray, bloke. Been making pies for the injured." She says calmly.

"Have to take a raincheck on the tea, Dorothy. Let's drag the chap into your flat, then I need to pop into his

flat for a bit. Let's hold off on calling the bobbies for now".
Jaime says.

"Can you keep an eye on him for a minute or two?"
Jaime asks knowing Wilhelm is no longer a threat.

"Sure! If he comes to, I'll whack him again." She assures
him. Jaime has no doubt she will.

Jaime turns the knob and finds Wilhelm's door is
locked. It's an old building and the door is easily pushed
open after a few powerful shoves. Dorothy watches over
Wilhelm as Jaime enters the small apartment. Its dark and
he fumbles for the chain switch of a replica tiffany lamp
on the table by the door.

The walls have faded wallpaper of large tropical flowers. In its day, it would have been fashionable and cheerful. 1920's tropical chic. But everything including the
worn carpet all belong to another time and have been
neglected. The flat has been left to age, uncared for by
the landlord.

Jaime quickly scours the apartment. He finds a suitcase, but it only contains rumbled clothing. It must be
here somewhere, he thinks. He lifts the old mattress,
opens every draw in the dresser, every cabinet door in
the tiny kitchenette. The closet only hold a few shirts and
pants on hangers. He stops and scans the two rooms over
and over, looking for something out of place.

Ahhhh, finally…... There it is! The faded tropical
flowers……they don't match up in a seam, stem and
flower are shifted slightly. He follows the break in the
pattern, and it forms a square at the bottom of the wall,
under the small kitchen table.

Jaime crawls on all fours and gives the wall a gentle push and the square easily dislodges. He reaches in and fishes around until his hand connects with the handle of a suitcase. It is unusually heavy. He quickly opens it to confirm its contents. "Bingo!" he whispers. He closes it and leaves the flat carrying the suitcase.

Dorothy is standing guard over Wilhelm. He is still out cold, and a patch of blood has dried on his forehead. Jaime reaches down to place two fingers on his neck to find a pulse. "He's alive….I need to ring someone up. Is there a phone box nearby?" Jaime asks.

"One right outside the front door on the street corner" Dorothy responds. "And yes, I'll stand guard."

Jaime runs down the stairs two steps at a time and allows himself chuckle. He marvels at Dorothy taking a break from her pie-making to take down a Nazi.

XXXIV. Greta's Fate

Greta has been allowed by British Intelligence to operate as a spy throughout the war. Without her knowing it, she has become more valuable to the British then she is to the Nazi's.

She will deliver countless messages to the Nazi's that contain false information, delivered to her by various 'double-cross agents'. But her days of being useful to the British have come to an end. Because the war is turning and it is believed the allies will be pushing ahead, Greta is now a flight risk.

One day after her rendezvous with Gustav Winter, Greta is escorted from her favorite haunt 'The Hope' to the 'The London Cage' located at the Kensington Palace Gardens. It is a temporary prisoner of war camp where Nazi spies are taken during the war.

Four days later after a hasty interrogation by the MI19 section of British Intelligence, Greta is sentenced to death by hanging. Greta is known as a notorious and dangerous spy reporting directly to Abwehr. There will be no arrangement brokered by the British to allow her to turn and in doing so, to live.

Accompanied by two guards, she stumbles to the gallows and begins her ascent to the top of the platform. She is wearing muddied dark red suede pumps and a smudge of matching lipstick that still remains on her soon to be silenced lips. Her beautiful eyes are marred by dark rings that have formed beneath them brought on by exhaustion, worry and sleepless nights. They are filled with tears that refuse to fall.

It is a dark and cloudy day in London. Rain starts to fall gently upon the grounds of the prison. Ravens have gathered where the hanging is about to take place, each vying for the best perch. An ominous sight. They communicate and seem to be chattering loudly of the unrest that has made its way to London once more. A city that has seen its share of upheavals and war-times…..it is once again the center of sorrow, struggle and unrest.

"Halt! Halt!" a guard yells as he runs out onto the gallows lawn. "Halt!" The man standing with Greta on the platform slowly removes the noose from her long delicate neck. Two guards rush forward and grab Greta under her arms. She slumps over in exhaustion and relief as they drag her away. Her legs seem to float as they remove her from the hastily built platform that would have held her last breath. The ravens take flight and circle the air above, waiting patiently for the next hanging.

The guards drag Greta back into 'The Cage' and down a long corridor. She is placed in a small room with a window facing out into the hallway. The guard hands her a glass of water. The water passes over her parched lips and down her throat. Water has never tasted so good. She lifts her tired head just in time to see Wilhelm being dragged in the direction she just came from. She knows for sure he will not be making the return trip.

Greta allows herself a smile, Jaime has found the note.

XXXV.   Sophie

As Jaime arrives home from his date with Greta, he reaches in his pocket to fish for the key to his flat. There he finds a carefully folded note. Greta must have slipped it into his pocket when he kissed her cheek. He unfolds it and reads.

My name is Sophie Händel, I am a Jew. I am originally from Berlin. I then made my way to Paris, before arriving in London. I am a double-agent working for the French Underground. I will now be attempting to flee, hopefully back to Paris to continue the fight. I know my days are numbered here in London and eventually I will be picked up by British Intelligence if I stay here. If I do get picked up before I leave, my story and I suppose my life are now in your hands. The only people who know of my disguise are working for the underground. I know you and I are working for the same side. I know this because as lovely as your almost perfect Berlin accent is, it has a touch of American in it. It has the most beautiful touch of American in it. …..and of course your swagger gave you away. Wilhelm was right all along, although I believe I convinced him he was mistaken.

Yours—Sophie

*P.S. Your valuable misinformation
was happily delivered to Wilhelm.*

Jaime spends two full days trying to convince Jonathan and the staff of MI5 that her note may hold truth. Indeed, she has been arrested and sent to the 'The Cage' as Jaime knew she would. Although she has tried to convince Intel at the London Cage of her allegiance to the same side, they are still convinced she is a Nazi spy. She has buried herself so deep in cover that it takes Jaime and British Intelligence another two days to find a member of the French Underground to substantiate her story. Her cover is so believable, she is willing to give up her life.

Jaime smiles as he realizes the outcome of his double-cross spy mission. He has saved one woman......but he has saved a woman who has in turn saved thousands of lives by putting her own life in danger every day. Sophie has been providing Wilhelm with false information since 1941. Sophie will live. She has chosen the right side of history.

XXXVI.   Rhodes-on-the-Pawtuxet

Gia still has not heard from Jaime. It has been a month since the D-Day invasion. She worries for him yet realizes he cannot communicate with her because of the classified mission he is on.

One night in early July, a few of the staff members decide to go to the Rhodes-on-the-Pawtuxet ballroom in Cranston, RI. Gia's roommate and friend Ruby believes this will cheer Gia up.

"You really need to get out and have some fun Gia, your mood is starting to make me blue......and that's pretty damn hard to do. Come on! Let's go cut a rug!" Ruby says with a giggle.

Gia declines. She remembers the last time she went dancing was with Jaime and can't imagine going out without him.

"Please! Pretty please, don't be a fuddy-duddy! It will be a gas!" Ruby coax's her to put on her white halter dress and pink gloves given to her by Jaime. Dressing up and dancing will lift her spirits.

"Ok, OK!" Gia relents.

Ruby and Gia sit in their shared room and get ready to go out. Ruby hands Gia a small glass of gin.

"This will loosen you up.....cheer up! We need a

fun night out!" Ruby says as she sits on the windowsill smoking a cigarette. She blows the smoke out the open window.

Ruby and Gia have become the best of friends. Ruby is a Chicago girl and they both share a 'city-girl' attitude. Ruby is street smart and quick witted. She has a knack for making Gia laugh. Tonight is no different and she soon has Gia giggling as they head out the door.

As they walk toward the ballroom, the music gets louder and louder. Sentimental Journey by Les Brown is playing.

Gia suddenly feels sad and nostalgic, thinking of Jaime. She regrets that she allowed Ruby to convince her to come. Her good spirits brought on by Ruby's humor have faded away. She feels guilty, out on the town, while Jaime is God knows where. She walks hesitantly until Ruby grabs her hand and pulls her toward the music.

"It's daiquiri night, dear! Makes me dance better! Makes everyone dance better! Let's go!" Ruby says.

As they enter the dance hall they all head to the bar to get a cocktail. As they get closer to the Rhodes bar, Gia takes a deep breath and her heart starts to pound....... for there is no mistaking the shoulders of the young man with his back to her standing at the bar.

Jaime swings around and grabs Gia by the waist and picks her up as if she is a feather. And all the worry, fear and doubt she has carried melts away....replaced by her tears of joy that fall onto the beautiful old, polished dance floor of the Rhodes-on-the-Pawtuxet ballroom.

Gia and her fellow workers all stand there staring at

Jaime in disbelief. They are all stunned. It's the first time Ruby is speechless since the beginning of the war.

"However, did you get here!?" Gia asks.

"I had an accomplice." Jamie replies.

"I thought you could all use a night out on me! You all deserve it! I couldn't have asked for a better crew!" Thomas Cave says as he strides up behind them. "I picked up this straggler at Union Station this afternoon. Brought along his smartest suit! Didn't want him meeting his girl and not looking his best!" He adds with a smile.

Thomas grabs Ruby's hand, and he leads her to the dance floor. Jaime grabs Gia's hand and leads her to the floor.

"Let's do it!" Jaime whispers in Gia's ear. "Let's get married!" he says as he presses something into Gia's hand. The North star pendant. "I told you I would carry it always. It brought me home to you." Jaime adds.

"Yes, yes….! Let's do it!" Gia replies as tears fall down her flushed cheeks.

They effortlessly shut the place down as the lights flicker on and off, a subtle way of letting them know it is time to hit the road. They all travel back to the station in a lighthearted mood, knowing there is a light at the end of the tunnel. The light is just around the bend, and it is getting brighter.

On a warm summer night in August of 1944, Gia and Jaime walk out of the Providence Courthouse husband and wife. Ruby and Thomas are the official witnesses.

Gia's family has made the trip from Brooklyn, including the lovely Gabrielle. Jaime's parents are there also.

Their first stop is dinner at Camille's.

They end the evening at the Alhambra Ballroom at Crescent Park. Of course, they all make a stop at the Carousel for a ride.

Gia tosses her bouquet from the painted wooden horse she rides, as the carousel turns. A young girl standing by the carousel catches it. She has the most beautiful golden locks swept up in a ponytail. She smiles and waves at Gia. She places the bouquet in a rusted red pail and skips away, blending into the crowd. Gia's gaze follows her as she disappears, wondering where she has seen her before.

XXXVII. Vive Paris

"Joelle! Joelle! You must come! You must come with me! It's happening! Finally! Camille says as she runs to the small attic room on the fourth floor and bangs on the door.

Joelle opens the door of her tiny bedroom. Camille is standing there flushed and smiling. She grabs Joelle's hand and pulls her toward the stairs.

"Come Joelle! Quickly! But first you must come to my boudoir. You have to put on one of my best dresses! It's the blue one you made for me! Come!" Camille says as she pulls Joelle down the stairs to her bedroom.

Camille opens her armoire and removes the dress. She hangs the beautiful blue dress on the dressing screen and motions Joelle to change into it. The dress is midnight blue silk with a matching lace mandarin collar. It is a sleeveless summer dress that fits tight to below the knees. Camille then hands Joelle blue silk pumps that match perfectly. "Lipstick!" Camille says as she hands her dark red lipstick to complete the transformation.

"Perfect, now let's go. Tout suite!" Camille says.

"What is happening?" Joelle asks.

"You must come outside!" Camille says.

"You know I cannot! Camille, what is happening?" asks Joelle.

"The allies have entered the city! Joelle, its over! The war is over! They are liberating Paris! Come!" Says Camille.

Camille and Joelle run all the way down to the first floor and run out into the streets. Gunshots are heard in the distance. There is still a small pocket of German resisters making their last stand, but they are swiftly quelled. People are running in all directions, yelling and laughing and singing.

"Vive France! Vive Paris!" the people shout with joy.

A group of people passing by, break into song. They are singing 'La Marseillaise' the national anthem of France.

"Come Joelle!" Camille grabs Joelle and they start to walk toward the Champs-Élysées.

This is the first time Joelle has been outside in three and a half years. It is late August 1944. The outside world seems surreal to Joelle. It's as if she were dreaming. She breathes deeply, taking in the air of her city. Taking in the old familiar smells, they are mixed with new ones that hold hints of smoke and gunpowder.

XXXVIII.   A Trusted Friend

On the night Joelle received the one and only letter from her daughter back in December of 1940, she heard shouting in the street.

"Stop, please! What are you doing!" a woman is screaming. Joelle stares out her bedroom window in disbelief. Helga Blath, Joelle's neighbor, is being dragged down the street by her hair. She is in the grips of a German officer.

"It is past curfew!" he screams at her. "Es-tu un juif? Es-tu un juif?" the officer asks.

"Say no." Joelle whispers to herself as she crouches lower to kneel at the window. She needs to avoid being seen. "Please! Please, say no!" Joelle repeats trying in vain to will the woman to deny she is Jewish.

"Oui, oui!" Helga answers.

He responds by pulling his gun out and promptly shoots Helga in the back of the head, still holding on to her hair. She goes limp. He lets go of her hair and she falls to the ground, blood forming a puddle under her blond curls. He leaves her there and walks away. He passes right below Joelle's window. Joelle looks to the other windows on her street and sees others watching. They pull their curtains together, afraid of being seen.

Joelle quietly walks down the stairs to street level and out the door. She walks over to Helga. She bends to check for a pulse, of course there is none. She hears a truck driving at full speed and looks up. It is headed straight for her. She manages to dash back up to her flat. The truck pulls up and two German soldiers jump out. They carry the body to the back of the truck and toss it in and drive away.

Joelle sits at her kitchen table shaking. It is time to go, she thinks. She packs a small bag with a few articles of clothing and her jewelry, tucking some photographs in as well. She uses her market bag, instead of a suitcase. She does this so she will not draw any attention to herself.

She dresses in her finest clothes and fixes her hair. She must avoid appearing bedraggled or anxious in any way. She is a Parisian woman, out to gather her rations for the day. She waits for the bells of Notre Dame Cathedral to signal it is eight o'clock in the morning. This is a reasonable time for a woman to start shopping for rationed items.

She knows of only one person she can trust entirely. Camille.

Joelle leaves her neighborhood and walks over the Seine using the Pont Neuf Bridge. She walks toward Les Halles, the marketplace. Then she takes a sharp left, and she walks past the Louvre, making her way to Rue St. Honoré. When she arrives at Camille's home she knocks softly on the door, but no one is at home. Joelle quickly crosses the street to the café she and Camille have frequented so many times. She sits and orders a café and waits.

One hour later, she sees Camille returning. Joelle leaves

change on the table and walks out. She walks slowly and calmly across the street.

When Camille sees her, she motions her to hurry.

"Oh, Thank God!" says Camille. "I just returned from your flat. I'm surprised we didn't pass each other on the way! I imagined the worst. Hurry, get inside. Tout suit!" She adds.

Joelle informs Camille what has happened right on her street.

"Dear God! Joelle, you must stay here! It is no longer safe. There is no going back now! I have the perfect space for you on the fourth floor." Camille says.

"Camille, how will I ever thank you! Saving Gabrielle, saving me." Joelle says.

"You are my best friend Joelle. Please, you don't have to thank me. I am so sorry for all you have been through. Come, let's sit and have a cup of coffee. Pierre has brought home the very best! I don't know how he got it!" says Camille trying to calm Joelle and herself for that matter. Each day brings a new horror, a new fear. How long can this go on? It can't possibly get any worse. But of course, it does.

Pierre, Camille and Joelle manage to move a twin bed up the narrow back staircase to the fourth floor. Camille and Joelle do the best they can to make the room comfortable and welcoming. Camille brings out her good linens and makes up the bed. She finishes it with a beautiful quilt. They fill the built-in shelves with books. Camille gives Joelle a sewing basket filled with everything she needs to hand sew and embroider.

At night Camille and Pierre slide an armoire across the back-stairway door on the second floor that leads to the third floor and to the attic. If there is a surprise search by the Nazi's it appears to be an ordinary wall at the back of the second-floor parlor. There is no back stairway leading from the first floor to the second, so anyone unfamiliar with the house would not notice anything out of place.

During the day Joelle is free to roam the entire house except for the first floor, she must avoid walking near all windows in the front of the house. It is a row house so there are only windows in the front and back. Camille shutters all of the back windows.

Joelle also hides when there are visitors. She can only trust Camille and Pierre.

"Joelle, I am so sorry….I'm afraid, for now, you must stop contacting Gabrielle for your own safety. They are censoring all mail in and out and it could lead the enemy to our doorstep. I'm so sorry, I know you understand." Camille explains. Eventually, the Nazi's will forbid any mail correspondence from Paris going to the United States and its allies.

"Of course, Camille. I understand." Joelle responds. Her heart is breaking, she yearns for both Gabrielle and Philip.

Joelle spends her days reading, embroidering, and writing letters to Gabrielle she will never send. They form a pile in a wooden box. She ties them in a ribbon Gabrielle wore in her hair as a little girl. Someday, she hopes….. Someday she will hand the box to her daughter.

At night, the three of them play cards by candlelight.

Some nights they tune into the BBC radio station from London, which is strictly forbidden by the Nazi's. They listen to Winston Churchill's inspiring speeches; his resilience and perseverance gives them hope. Churchill vows to fight out the war to the finish, never surrendering to the Nazis.

One night while listening, they learn that the allies have landed in Normandy. In celebration, Pierre opens a bottle of Chateau Lafite de Rothchild, he has hidden in the cellar behind the furnace. They sip it slowly, enjoying a rare extravagance in the midst of despoliation.

They continue to listen to the BBC religiously after that glorious piece of news passes over the airwaves. They all await the liberation with cautious joy. Counting the hours, counting the days. The allies have come by sea. The allies are on the march. The allies are in the air......and the allies are headed straight for Paris.

Finally, the day has come. Camille brings Joelle out into the streets, her first day of freedom in so long.

De Gaulle enters Paris first with the French soldiers. De Gaulle is defiant of the remaining pockets of Germans soldiers still resisting and vows to make it all the way to Notre Dame. The people of the city are celebrating wildly in the streets.

The next day the allies march in, including the Americans. What a sight it is to behold. Camille, Joelle, and Pierre maneuver to the front of the crowd. The Americans are marching twenty-three across, taking up the entire width of the Champs-Élysées. There are more Americans marching in to liberate Paris than there were

German soldiers that marched in to invade the city four years ago. The American soldiers smile as the march in, full of hope and joy. So in contrast to the faces of the German soldiers when they marched in.

The cheers for the American soldiers are deafening. Joelle cheers along. She feels extraordinary admiration and fondness for these battle worn troops so far away from home, marching in to liberate her city. She also feels a deep affinity for the Americans, knowing her daughter lives amongst them now. She smiles at the thought, Gabrielle in America. She can finally write to her; be sure she is still safe. Her cheers mix with her tears of hope and relief.

It is over, finally over. Now Joelle will wait for Philip. Surely, he will come home soon, and they will be able to join Gabrielle.

A week later when the city begins to calm somewhat, Joelle tells Camille she would like to walk to her apartment. It is time to go home.

"Yes! Let's go! Pierre and I will join you!" Camille says.

The three of them walk through the Paris streets. They are crowded with revelers and others heading to the market in search of any provisions that may be available. The city is in transition and food supplies are extremely low. Joelle wonders how quickly food supplies will be brought into the city, to feed the thousands of hungry Parisians. She is so grateful to have Camille and Pierre. Having various connections, they have survived the war with an adequate amount of food and drink. Most of the citizens of Paris have gone without for four years and it will take time before there is a return to normalcy.

When they arrive, Joelle enters the apartment first. It is time capsule of December 1940. A thin white layer of dust covers everything, as if a flurry of snow has magically fallen from the ceiling above in her absence. Someone has been inside, foraging for food. Joelle smiles, wanting to meet this thoughtful thief who only came to visit out of hunger. Only the sparse amount of food Joelle had when she left is gone.

Everything else in the apartment is untouched, just as she left it. Her clothes are still strewn about, reminding her of the urgency and fear she felt on that December night.

"I think it is time I returned home for good, Philip should be returning soon now that the prisoners have been released. I should be here when he arrives." Joelle says with guarded optimism.

"Well then, let's get going! Pierre, you are excused for the day! Joelle and I will spend the day getting this place back in order." Camille says as she playfully pushes Pierre out the door.

"Au revoir Mesdames! Have a lovely day of cleaning!" Pierre winks at Joelle and Camille as he leaves.

Joelle and Camille work all day, dusting, scrubbing, and putting everything back into place.

In the late afternoon Joelle hears a soft knock on the door. She opens the door to see her neighbor, Paul Armand. He is an older man, in his late seventies. He is holding a warm French baguette wrapped in paper.

"This is for you Madame. I'm afraid I owe you an apology. I am the thief who took the pleasure of relieving you of your food supply." He says with a smile as he hands Joelle the baguette.

"While you were away a bedraggled French soldier came to your door delivering a small pouch. He came to your door two days in a row, on the third day he came and knocked on my door. He told me he could not stay another day; he was making his way back home. He had somehow escaped while on a march east with other French prisoners. They were marching to a camp located deeper into Germany. He took great risk entering Paris to deliver this pouch. He made me promise I would deliver it only to you. I have held on to it for two years." Paul explains as he hands her the small worn drawstring leather pouch.

"Why, whatever is it. What is inside?" Joelle asks

"I don't know. He also made me promise that the contents were for your eyes only. So I am not privy to what it contains. I kept my promise. I am happy to see you are well and made it through the blasted war unscathed! Well, perhaps not unscathed, we will all be forever wounded. If only in our hearts. I should say…. I'm happy you made it through alive. Welcome home!" Paul says and then he turns and departs.

Joelle walks slowly to her couch and sits. Camille follows. Joelle is hesitant; she opens the pouch slowly and tips it to empty the contents. Her heart sinks as she hears the gentle clink on the coffee table in front of her. She looks down, already knowing what has made the sound, already knowing what has fallen before her. Philip's wedding ring rolls in a complete circle before coming to a stop before her. She stares at it, then she reaches and picks it up and slides it onto her finger….. willing it to fit her slender ring finger. But, of course, it is too large. She squeezes it in the palm of her hand so hard it makes a temporary imprint.

She then reaches back into the pouch and pulls out a yellowed and water-stained piece of paper, folded into a perfect square. The handwriting on the paper is unmistakable. '*À mon cœur, À mon amour, Pour ma vie.*' Is written on the outside. Camille wraps her arms around Joelle as they both begin to cry. Joelle's cry is guttural, from deep inside. It has been held there for a very long time, now it is time to release it. It is time to release the bottled-up pain and sorrow that has been stored up just for this very moment.

In her heart, Joelle has always known he was gone. She could feel it. Yet, she held on to the hope her feelings were deceiving her. Her intuition has always been her truth. Her instinct her mightiest strength.

Joelle slowly unfolds the piece of paper to read the last letter that Philip will ever write.

'*My dearest Joelle, if you are reading this I am gone, my love. Typhus runs rampart in this prison and I'm afraid it has made its way to me. My prison mate Eugene promised me he would get this letter to you. Although my life has been much too brief, take heart my dear. I would not have changed a bit of it. I die considering myself the most fortunate of men, because I have had you as my love and as my precious wife. And then came our bright and beautiful Gabrielle to make us complete. I know*

*you are both safe, because you are fierce my dear, a fierce
lion of a Mama to our dear daughter. You will pro-
tect our most beautiful creation. You must believe that
I am not gone completely, Joelle. I sit beside you now,
to wipe your tears away. Grieve for me? Yes, of course
or I will haunt you! But do not grieve for me too long.
Speak of me. Speak of me with Gabrielle every day and
remember the wonderful times we had together, mon
cœur. It will keep me alive, for I will never leave you.
Take a walk on the banks of the Seine and sit where we
picnicked so many years ago. You know the spot! And
call my name and I will answer you! Someday we will
reunite, I am sure of it . . . . . . I wait patiently to hold you
once again in my arms. Live a full and wonderful life
for me, Joelle. Carry me along on all of your wonderful
adventures. Think of me just before you drift off to sleep
every night. Remember, my love for you and Gabrielle
will live on forever. Je t'aime toujours. Philip*

Joelle slumps and her head falls onto Camille's lap.
Camille runs her hand over Joelle's hair, in an attempt to
comfort her. But there is no comfort to be had. It is time
to grieve.

'How much can Joelle take' Camille thinks. 'How
much can this poor woman take.'

Camille contemplates that there must be thousands of
these letters of final goodbyes making their way to loved
ones all across France, all across Europe, all across America…...all across the world for that matter. They all speak
of love, because that is all there is in the end.

"Joelle, we must get a letter to Gabrielle. She must know he is gone, but she must also know that you are not! She must know that you have survived!" Camille says.

"Yes, yes I know. How do I tell her Camille? How do I tell Gabrielle her Papa is gone." Joelle whispers.

"You will find the words, as only a mother can." Says Camille.

Joelle decides to write to her cousin Samuel and break the news to him. Inside the letter to Samuel, she will tuck a letter to Gabrielle. Samuel will be able to prepare and comfort her. She posts the letter.

She checks her mail everyday knowing it could take weeks, maybe months for post war mail to make its way across the Atlantic.

As much as she tries, Joelle cannot shake her sadness. She must get back on her feet and start to earn a living. Her goal is to save enough money to secure passage to the United States when it is safe to travel again.

XXXIX.   April in New York

It has been months since Gabrielle learned of her father's death. Her great sorrow is mixed with the joy of knowing her mother has made it through the war alive. Paris has been liberated and is on the mend, returning to its former glory.

In the letter, Joelle tells Gabrielle how Camille saved her life. She describes how Camille put herself and Pierre in danger by doing so.

Gabrielle misses her mother terribly. She continues her studies, walking to Brooklyn College every day. She writes to her Mama urging her to come to America. But she knows her mother is trying her best to save the money needed to make the journey. 'All in good time, soon we will be together!' her Mama promises in her reply's.

Gabrielle sees Joey every day. He is also enrolled at Brooklyn College, so some days they walk there together. Joey is majoring in History and Education. He hopes to become a teacher.

Joey now walks with a cane, finally putting the crutches aside for good. The slow walks to the college allow for long conversations between the two of them. Joey is certain that Gabrielle is the one. He hopes she feels the same about him.

The war has had a profound effect on Joey, changing his focus on how he would like to spend his life.

"Those who cannot remember the past are condemned to repeat it." Joey quotes George Santayana when explaining his reasons for choosing a career as a history teacher.

"I'm hoping I can educate the young to believe that no good can possibly come out of war." He adds as he walks with Gabrielle. He has one hand on his cane, the other holds Gabrielle's hand. He carries his books in an old leather satchel thrown over his shoulder.

"Oui, I understand. Il est a noble profession!" Says Gabrielle. Joey loves the way she now combines both the French and English language in most sentences. As she learns the English language, Joey learns the French language in return. Each day brings them closer as they learn to communicate, each trying so hard to learn the others language.

They make quite a pair. Gabrielle is tall and thin, elegant and beautiful. Her hair is long, she wears it parted on the side and held back by a tortoise shell barrette her mother bought for her in Paris. Her hair ends in curls that hang down her back. Her eyes are wide and blue. She is serious, reflecting a life interrupted. But when she laughs, it is contagious because of its authenticity.

Joey is undeniably handsome. His features are Roman. Large brown eyes, a straight prominent nose, a square dimpled chin. Although not tall, his proportionate physique is statuesque. When he walks beside Gabrielle, they are almost the same height.

As they walk down the street together, eyes follow

them as they pass by. It is as if they just walked off a Hollywood movie set. They make a stunning pair. They belong together. They fit naturally together, as if she was destined to make the journey to Brooklyn and he was meant to live in the apartment just above her.

Joey still works at the corner store with his mother and father, his job is lead baker. Half of his time is spent covered in flour, the other half is spent in a wonderful mixture of Gabrielle and academics. Joey starts to save his money with a purpose in mind.

The war is slowly coming to an end as the allies push through Europe. They liberate those who have been held captive and have miraculously lived to speak of the horrors. The world begins to learn of the unthinkable atrocities the Nazi's have committed.

Gabrielle and Joey are in their usual spot, sitting in the window seat at her uncle's apartment. This is where they do their reading and studies each afternoon. It is early April of 1945.

"You too academics need to take a break! Tomorrow is Sunday, a good day to take in some sights!" says Uncle Samuel. "Let's have a family day in Manhattan, a picnic in Central Park! You must come too Joseph!" Samuel adds as he winks at Joey. Joey has become a permanent fixture at the Levy household. Samuel has taken a liking to this hard-working young man and he realizes how much Joey cares for Gabrielle. The excursion includes Martine, Chloe, Samuel, Gabrielle and Joey.

The next day they head out, taking the subway and trolley to Central Park. It is a beautiful April day. Samuel and Martine have packed a picnic basket filled with wine, cheeses, and bread. Joey brings a box of freshly baked pastry from the bakery. They lay down two blankets in the Central Park grass. It is a perfect day to take in the sun after the long winter. Flowers are making their first appearances of the season in the park.

"Let's take a walk to the harbor and see the ships come in!" Samuel suggests after they finish their picnic lunch. After packing the empty plates and wine glasses into a basket, they all head toward the New York Piers. Is a half an hour walk down 60th Street to reach the harbor.

The gigantic piers are lined up, reaching into the Hudson River. Massive ships float in and out. Some bring cargo, many bring passengers from all over the world. Some are refugees from war torn Europe. Their decks are filled to capacity with weary travelers and American troops returning from Europe.

They all settle on a bench and watch in amazement as the large ships maneuver, barely missing each other as they dock and depart.

"Come, let's take a closer look. Look at the Queen Mary coming in to dock. Isn't it spectacular!" Samuel says. They all follow his lead and walk over to this massive ship. It is truly magnificent.

"Gabrielle, come see! Look up! Let's wave to the passengers!" Joey says.

Gabrielle looks up at the crowded deck. Women, men, children, and American troops all waving and yelling. It is a sight to behold, they are refugees who have made their way to America from various parts of Europe. A swarm of old woolen coats fill the deck, some with patches sewn on at the elbows. Their faces hold the joy of a second chance at life. This is America and they are breathing in the smoky New York Harbor air. It smells of freedom.

At first Gabrielle cannot comprehend what she is hearing.

"Gabrielle! Gabrielle!" she hears someone calling from far above her on the deck of the ship. The voice competes with all the other shouting voices, it fades in and out. "Gabrielle!." She hears it again.

Gabrielle looks up and scans the deck, the sun blinds her. She puts her hand above her eyes, squinting toward the deck of the ship. 'Where is it coming from?! Where?! It cannot be!' Gabrielle thinks as she scans the deck. "It simply cannot be!.'

"Joey! Cousin Samuel! I can hear! I can hear my name being called! It sounds like my momma! It cannot be! Where?!" Gabrielle is frantic.

"There!" Samuel points. "There!" he yells.

And then Gabrielle sees her. She is leaning over the rail, making her way to the gangplank. It cannot be, yet it is. She is in the midst of hundreds of passengers hurrying to disembark. All in a haste to get onto the dock and onto American soil for good. Many are hurrying to get to a loved one waiting below.

Gabrielle pushes her way through the crowd. Tears are clouding her vision. Joelle is pushing her way to the gangplank. It is a chaotic cluster of smiling, laughing, joyful people all moving, it seems, as a single mass. All connected by their collective relief of a journeys end in a place where they are welcome and safe.

Gabrielle and Joelle keep their eyes on each other as they move toward each other. Gabrielle is afraid to take her eyes off her mother, fearing she may disappear. Is it all a dream? Minutes go by, they are closer and closer. And then they are in each other's arms. They hold on to each other for a while, not believing it is true. They are together again, after so long.

Joelle loosens her hold on Gabrielle, to look around at the small group that has gathered around them.

"Samuel….. Martine! And this must be Chloe!" Joelle says through her tears. They all embrace her one by one.

"And Joseph! Is this the wonderful young man that has stolen my daughter's heart?" Joelle asks already knowing the answer.

Joey walks up to Joelle and they embrace. She takes his head in her hands and kisses both his cheeks.

"Let's go home! You are home now, Joelle! It is time to go home. " Samuel says.

They all make their way back to Brooklyn. Martine makes tea and brings out more of Joey's pastries on a china platter. Joelle and Gabrielle settle on the couch, holding hands, not wanting to let go of each other.

"Mama, how did you get here? How? Tell me everything!" asks Gabrielle.

"Well, mon cher! I will tell you the story of how I got here. It is a story with a very happy ending." Joelle says. And then she begins to tell her story.

XL. The Ritz

Paris is once again a free city and on the mend. It is March of 1945. Joelle has put her dress shop back together, with Camille's help. She has a few returning customers. Most come to have worn clothes mended. They are all trying to restore some sort of normalcy to a very broken world.

Joelle puts any money earned into a jar. Her home is with her daughter in America. She is not sure how long it will take, but that is her goal.

Camille visits her every day, each time bringing an item that is still coveted by a city of rationed goods. It is taking some time for Paris to regain its food supply.

Joelle is mending a child's coat. It is powder blue wool, with a white fur collar. Paisley silk lining. She thinks of Gabrielle as a child. 'Didn't she have one just like this?' Joelle thinks. She goes to Gabrielle's tiny bedroom and looks through her closet. There it is, but it is a coat of pale violet, with a cream fur collar. She brings it to her face, trying to find the scent of Gabrielle buried in the wool. It is fading, but it lingers there still. Joelle sits on Gabrielle's twin bed, neatly made up. It is as if at any moment Joelle will hear the familiar footsteps of Gabrielle running up the stairs, coming home from school. 'How long will it

149

take, Joelle ponders. How long will it take to save enough to make her way to America?'

On an unusually warm March day, Joelle hears the familiar knock on the door. She opens the door to Camille. It is Joelle's favorite time of the day.

"Good afternoon Madame! It is time to get you out for a nice dinner! Get dressed! Tout suit!" Camille says as she claps her hands together.

"Where are we going? What should I where?" asks Joelle.

"The Ritz, mon cher! And you know what to wear, you have dressed half the women of Paris in your beautiful creations." Camille says with her beautiful wide smile.

Joelle scans her closet, ah there it is! A beautiful cream silk dress. A high mandarin collar of intricate ribbon work done in black. Belle sleeves that fall slightly over her hands, embellished with the same black ribbon work. Joelle made it for a wealthy client just before the occupation. As luck would have it, her client never returned to fetch it. Now she will wear it to The Ritz. She slips it over her head, feeling the cool fabric come to rest on her slim figure. They have all lost weight over the past four years due to constant fear and heavy rationing. Camille and Joelle work together to fix her hair up into a French twist. Camille reaches in her purse and pulls out pearl earrings and all of the cosmetics she could fit to make up Joelle's lovely face.

"Parfait! Vous êtes une vision!" Camille exclaims as she grabs Joelle's hands, and they spin as if dancing. Joelle's spirits are lifted by the frivolity of the moment.

They put on their light spring coats and gloves and start their long walk to The Ritz. It is a beautiful day. Over the Seine and past the Louvre, they walk hand in hand. Dear old friends, smiling and chatting along the way. It seems the whole city of Paris is smiling.

As they walk into the lobby of The Ritz, Pierre is there to greet them. It is just as beautiful as she remembers when she visited so many years ago on a date with Philip. It was their first wedding anniversary; it seems like another life. A life she now misses and envies. Did she realize back then how fortunate she was? Or did she take it all for granted?

She takes in the beauty that surrounds her. The towering flower arrangements, the brocade settee's, the gold gilded mirrors. It appears The Ritz has made it through the occupation completely unchanged. She reasons the Nazi Officers that inhabited it during the war demanded it remain the same to support their self-centered wants and needs. Only the best for them, while the citizens of Paris starved.

"Ah! Les deux plus belles femmes de Paris!" Pierre exclaims.

He leads them into the dining room. It is bustling with customers. Paris is coming back to life. Pierre guides Camille and Joelle to a table. A gentleman sits there waiting. The room is decorated in gold and pink. The walls are covered in gold patterned silk. The chairs are covered in pink brocade, the table clothes and linens all white. Again, the room is filled with flower arrangements that reach for the ceiling.

Pierre makes the introductions. "Camille, Joelle this is Thomas Jordan. A diplomat from the U.S. Embassy."

"En chante!" Thomas says.

The four sit and make small talk for a while. They order wine and hors d'oeuvres to start. Escargot…..It has been a long time since Joelle has tasted something so delicious! So decadent! The conversation remains light throughout dinner. They all enjoy the exceptional cuisine. After dinner, over coffee and a tray of sweets, the conversation changes.

"Joelle, it seems you have quite an assemblage of people concerned for your well-being in the United States and here in France." Thomas says.

"Pardon?" replies Joelle.

"One Samuel and Martine Levy of Brooklyn New York?……. and Joseph Franzese? I believe the latter is a friend of your daughter Gabrielle. And then of course Camille and Pierre. All planning and scheming behind your back to ensure your happiness. You are much loved Joelle. Much loved." Thomas says with a warm smile.

Joelle nods in agreement and then tilts her head in question, not knowing what this could be about. She remains speechless, allowing for an explanation.

Thomas then passes Joelle an envelope. Joelle is bewildered as she slowly opens the envelope.

"It is your papers and passage to America. It is safe to travel now. The whole world is on the move. Everyone is making their way home or to a new home. War does that. It has a tendency to relocate people." Thomas reveals.

Everyone at the table falls silent. Joelle is so overcome,

she cannot speak. So, they all wait for her to absorb the information…..they allow her to get a grasp on what is happening. Camille reaches and grabs her hand.

"How? How?" is all Joelle can get out. Her tears fall unchecked, dotting her beautiful cream silk dress.

"They have all arranged this for you Joelle. It is time for you to reunite with your daughter. Your home is now in the United States. All is arranged. You leave on March 30th. You will be traveling on the Queen Mary. You will have to make your first journey to Southampton, England where the ship is docked. You will arrive at the port of New York on April 4th" Thomas says.

"How can I ever thank all of you? It is too much……" Joelle voice trails off to silence. She has no words. It is all too much.

"You can thank us by joining your daughter, mon cher! Gabrielle needs her mother, and you need your daughter. Thank us by living a full life in America! It is time to find your happiness Joelle and it lies across the Atlantic!" says Camille.

They finish the evening with a bottle of champagne.

"À Joelle! Mon très cher ami! Un bon voyage en Amérique!" says Camille, already missing her dear friend. Wondering what she will do without her.

They all raise their glasses. And the glasses clink. And the laughter is loud. And Paris has witnessed the last time Joelle's tears will fall in this beloved city. Joelle will only take the good memories with her on her journey. Memories of the blissful days spent with Philip and Gabrielle before the war. Memories of afternoon teatime spent with Camille when lemons were plentiful.

She will leave her sorrows here in this ancient city, as her fellow Parisians struggle to comprehend what truly happened in the city of light and why it was allowed to happen by so many of its own.

XLI.   A Wedding in Brooklyn

Jaime and Gia run through the train station, laughing as they make their way to the train. They are running late and barely step on the train as it departs Providence for Grand Central Station, New York City.

It is late September of 1945. The war is officially over. The country is celebrating. The young are getting married, buying houses and having babies.

"I can't believe it! My little brother getting married! And to a beautiful Parisian!" Gia says with a smile. Jaime and Gia sit side by side on the train, Gia's head leans gently on Jaime's shoulder and she is lulled to sleep by the rocking of the train. It has been quite a year.

Their positions at the Chopmist Hill listening post have come to an end. They have purchased a small Victorian cottage on the water in Riverside, Rhode Island within walking distance of Crescent Park. They discover the house while visiting the park. In total disrepair, Jaime and Gia are able to purchase the house for a song.

Jaime currently works at an Architecture firm in Providence, while attending night school at the University of Rhode Island. Gia attends night classes at Rhode Island School of Design, while working at Shephard's department store during the day.

Their weekends are spent together. They are slowly restoring the cottage back to its original splendor. They scour antique stores salvaging old doors, windows and gingerbread trim. It has been a blissful year together.

They step off the train in New York and are greeted by Joey and Gia's father, Anthony. The women are all at home making preparations for the wedding.

XLII.   Something Blue

It is the night before the wedding. Gabrielle and Chloe have decided that the women will be spending the night together without the men. Gabrielle will not see Joey until she walks down the aisle.

"Come on Mama! We are all going to Manhattan. First is dinner at a small French restaurant called Le Veau d'or. I've heard it is the most authentic French food! Just like Paris! Then perhaps some music!" Gabrielle says. She is excited to show her Mama around Manhattan. The six women dress up for the evening and Gabrielle calls two cabs to take them into the city.

They all settle in at Le Veau d'Or for dinner to start the dinner. They are giddy with laughter. Joelle starts with Soupe A L'oignon Gratinee.

"Ah! C'est délicieux!" Joelle says and winks at Gabrielle. They all order Canard à la sauce Aux Cerises, the best in Manhattan. Joelle and Gabrielle share Parfait au rhum for dessert, with a cup of café.

"It is time for a bit of music before we go home." Gabrielle says and they jump in the cabs and they head to Greenwich Village.

The cabs stop in front of the Café Society. It is a new and popular club featuring the best blues and jazz musicians in the country.

When they enter, the nightclub is jammed with people. There is a special guest playing tonight, but apparently word has gotten out that it is someone quite famous. Gabrielle manages to secure a table up on the balcony.

When they get settled, they all order a drink. The first act is The Golden Gate Quartet. Once regulars at the Café Society, it is their first appearance in five years. The crowd goes crazy when they walk on stage. Their last song is 'Joshua Fit The Battle of Jericho'. The crowd sings along.

After a short intermission, the lights are dimmed the lowest they can possibly go.

"I wonder who the special guest is?" Joelle leans in to ask Gabrielle.

"I have no idea, but it must be someone big! Its standing room only now!" Gabrielle says, but she already knows who it is. It is the reason she planned her wedding on this particular weekend. She has known for weeks. It is her wedding gift to her mother. Something blue for the mother-of-the-bride. She smiles to herself, hardly able to contain her excitement.

The announcer makes his way to the stage and the crowd goes silent.

"Ladies and Gentlemen, please welcome to the stage the one and only Billie Holiday!" he says.

The cheers in the room are deafening. Everyone is standing and cheering.

Joelle grabs Gabrielle hand, her eyes well with tears and her face an expression of disbelief. She is speechless.

Billie Holiday makes her way to the stage. She is wearing her hair swept up, with two white gardenia's tucked into her hair. She is stunning, wearing a cream satin dress that reaches the floor.

She starts her set with 'God Bless the Child'. It is the song Joelle played over and over in her attic room hideaway in Paris. When she wore the record out, Camille spent weeks before she could locate another one for Joelle.

The audience is so transfixed they cannot sit down. She continues to sing all of her popular standards. Joelle knows every word of every song.

It is her last song. The nightclub goes completely dark, with the exception of a spotlight on Billie Holiday's face. She sings 'Strange Fruit'. The painfully haunting song mesmerizes the audience. When the song is over the entire club goes completely dark. The audience is hushed by the unexpected darkness. When the lights come back on, Billie Holiday is gone, leaving the audience to contemplate what they have just heard.

It is an unforgettable evening. It is time to go home.

Gabrielle and Joelle have been sharing a small bedroom in Samuel's apartment since Joelle arrived. When they get home, they both fall into bed exhausted. After a few minutes of reliving the evening with talk and suppressed laughter, they manage to drift off to sleep.

They both awaken at the same time, sleeping later than they expected because of their late evening. They look at each other and start to giggle all over again.

"Oh my beautiful girl! Today is your day! This is the last morning I will see my little girl as a 'Mademoiselle, you will soon be known as Madame Frazese!" and they both continue to giggle.

"Up! Up mon amour! Tout suit! It is time to prepare!" Joelle says. They both roll out of bed and put their robes on. Martine has made a fresh pot of coffee, and the glorious smell has made its way to the bedroom they share.

Chloe stands at the dining room table sipping her coffee while she arranges special pastries on a bone china platter. Joelle reaches for a Rugelach, thinking of Camille and their afternoon teas together. She misses her dear friend.

"Bonjour ma belle mariée! Chloe says as she runs to Gabrielle and hugs her. Chloe and Gabrielle have grown so close, they are like sisters.

"I have thrown Samuel out for the day." Martine says in jest. "Today is to be spent with just the ladies! We will see the men at the chapel this afternoon!" she adds.

There is a soft knock at the door.

"Ah, that will be Gia and Angela!" Martine informs them.

Gia and Angela enter also wearing their morning robes. They carry the dresses they will be wearing to the wedding. They all settle down at the dining room table and enjoy a rare Saturday morning without the men, feasting on special pastries made just for this occasion. They talk of dresses and flowers, hairstyles and lipstick and of course, honeymoon nights. It is a perfect morning.

After breakfast the women move to the living room. Joelle is sitting on the sofa stitching Gabrielle's dress.

Gabrielle has decided she wants a fashionable dress instead of a gown. Joelle is taking it in at the waist.

"The bride always loses weight right before the wedding. It never fails. I am always stitching right up until the bride walks down the aisle. Nerves!" Joelle says. She spreads the dress out over the sofa to examine it. They all gather to look at it. It is beautiful. Handmade by Joelle, it has taken her two months to finish. The top above the bust and the sleeves are made from fine cream-colored French lace. The lace dips slightly at the cleavage. The rest of the dress is made of cream silk. It is fitted all the way to just below the knee to accentuate Gabrielle's tall and slender figure.

They spend the day primping and lounging. They all fawn over Gabrielle. She blushes at the attention. Finally, all the hair is done up, the lipstick put on.

They all put on their dresses, saving the bride for last.

"Come Gabrielle, it is time!" Joelle says holding the dress.

Joelle slips the dress over Gabrielle's head, and it falls, gracefully covering her body. They all stand back to observe. She is a vision.

"Parfait! Tu est parfait! You need one more addition! Something blue! You need something blue to wear! It is tradition! Blue will bring a marriage filled with love!" Joelle says.

"Chloe! Can you bring me my old brown leather shoes? The ones I wore on the ship traveling here." Joelle says. They all stop talking, wondering why Joelle would want her old shoes at this particular moment.

Chloe returns with the shoes and hands them to Joelle.

"Martine, does Samuel own a screwdriver by chance?" Joelle asks.

"Why yes Joelle! But why in heavens name would you need a screwdriver?" Martine asks.

"Just bring it to me, s'il vous plait!" Joelle demands.

Martine retrieves the screwdriver from the bottom kitchen draw and hands it to Joelle.

They all watch in disbelief and wonder as Joelle pries the bottom of a shoe heel off one of her old brown shoes. She then removes a small black velvet pouch from the inside of the heel.

"Mama! What is that? Mama, what in the world is that?" Gabrielle asks with a look of puzzlement.

They have all gathered around Joelle and they are staring down at the tiny black velvet pouch with the name Cartier embossed on it.

"Mon chérie, mon amour!" Joelle says as she looks into her daughter's eyes.

"How could I ever risk your grandmother's sapphire and diamond earrings getting into the hands of those Nazi bastards! The earrings have been hidden in my shoe since the day they entered Paris!" Joelle says with a conspiratorial giggle.

Gabrielle is speechless. Not only because her mother has smuggled the earrings to America in her shoe, but because she has never heard her mother swear until this very moment.

"Well, I'll be!" Martine says in amazement. The others remain silent, awed by what they have just witnessed.

Joelle shakes the earrings out of the pouch and into her hand. They are perfect emerald cut blue sapphires. The perfect color…, the perfect cut….. they are surrounded by tiny diamonds. They sit in an intricate filigree art nouveau setting of platinum.

"Come sit next to me. Your Grandmama wore these at her wedding, then I wore them at mine. Now it is your turn mon Coeur." Joelle says as she pats the space next to her on the settee. Gabrielle sits and Joelle clips the earrings onto her ears.

"Stand for us, ma belle fille." she adds.

Gabrielle stands before them. She is perfect. The earrings sparkle brightly, as if approving of their new home in America.

Martine and Chloe bring out champagne and glasses. They all raise their glasses.

"To Gabrielle and Joey!" and they all clink their glasses.

"It is time to go! The car is here!" Martine says as she peeks out the window to the street below. Samuel has arranged to have the women picked up in a flashy car. They all make their way down the stairs, and they spill out onto the sidewalk, laughing with excitement as they go.

They make their way to a small stone chapel tucked between the tenements that line the street. It is one of the oldest churches in Brooklyn. The men have all arrived and wait patiently inside. It is a small family wedding.

The women step into the chapel leaving Gabrielle and Chloe outside, holding their bouquets of lilies and forget-me-nots. Then the organ music starts to play the

Mendelssohn's wedding march. Chloe enters as maid of honor. Then Gabrielle enters. Joey stands at the altar, leaning on his cane, tears well up in his eyes. She is so beautiful. She is his everything.

All eyes are on Gabrielle as she makes her way down the aisle to the alter. The tears that flow are a combination of joy, love and shear wonder. This Parisian girl, this Brooklyn boy. So very different. They are brought together by the destiny that America has offered them.

A rabbi and priest officiate the wedding. Then they are off to Bamonte's Italian restaurant for a meal that lasts for hours. Platters of all their favorite Italian dishes are brought to the table. The meal is followed by a wedding cake and spumoni. The dinner is filled with laughter and countless kisses between Gabrielle and Joey, in response to the clinking of glasses.

XLIII. Copacabana

The night is young, and it calls to the young newly-weds. The older adults make their way home as the young ones make their way to the waiting car and head to the Copacabana. Opening in 1940, it is the hottest club in New York City.

"Joey, how are we going to get in? It's impossible! Lines around the block!" Gia says knowing the Copacabana's reputation.

"The manager of the club stops by the bakery every Friday and Saturday for three boxes of pastries. He brings it in for all of his employees, including the showgirls! So, we've become pretty tight. He reserved a table close to the front! Of course, I have promised him what amounts to a year's worth of free pastry! Don't tell Mom or Pop!" Joey explains and they all break into laughter.

When they arrive, Joey approaches the man standing behind the black velvet ropes at the front door of the club and whispers in his ear. The man unhooks the rope and motions them in with a quick nod. Joey grabs Gabrielle's hand and the rest follow him in. He then approaches the maître d who in turn quickly scans the list.

"Table 25" he says to the hostess, and she motions them to follow. They follow the smart looking hostess. She is dressed in a tight-fitting black satin strapless dress. Her silver gloves reach past her elbow to her upper arms. Her auburn hair is swept up into a French twist held by rhinestone clips. She walks confidently in three-inch pumps that are covered in silver beads.

"I've never seen anything like this! It's beautiful1" says Chloe. The room is a combination of mirrors and ornate decorations. A sweeping curtain of fuchsia and white temporarily hides the stage. The band-stand boxes are all hand painted the same, an exotic woman wearing a turban headband covered with flowers.

They can hardly hear each other, the conversation and music in the room is so loud. Soon the curtains slowly open and the beautiful showgirls make their way to the stage. The music has a strong Latin beat. The dancers wear shear skirts of gold lame with scant shorts underneath. They wear shiny gold beaded bra's, their midriffs bare. The gold and white feather headpieces are over two feet high. It is a dreamy spectacle, filled with exotic and sensual excitement.

The waitress are so busy, Jaime and Joey decide to head to the bar to get the drinks for the table.

The place is jammed. Jaime and Joey have to weave their way to the bar. The bartender is busy making elaborately mixed tropical drink's, some pass by in ceramic coconut and pineapple shaped vessels, all garnished with fresh fruit. Jaime places their order. They realize they will be waiting for quite a while. The three bartenders are trying to keep up with the orders passing drinks left and right, spilling the overflow onto a sticky mirrored bar. They are laughing and chatting with every customer as they work feverishly to keep up the relentless pace. They weave and spin past each other, avoiding near misses as they deliver the drinks. A seamless pirouette of the bartenders.

Jaime turns and leans on the bar. He takes the time to gaze around the room. Post war America. A time of peace has finally settled in. Lovers who made wartime promises dance as husbands and wives. Laughter and joy fills the room.

Jaime smiles and turns back to the bar as one of the bartenders finally slides the drinks towards them.

"These are on the beautiful dark-haired dame at the end of the bar" the bartender says as he tilts his head to Jaime's left.

Jaime turns to follow his lead. He cannot believe his eyes. He is looking at the beautiful face of Greta. Gone is the heavy made-up face of a spy undercover. Her face is also free of the stresses of her former occupation. She looks like a young girl, excited to be out on the town. She lifts her glass to toast Jaime from her end of the bar and offers an unabashed and gorgeous smile.

"I'll meet you back at the table! I need to say 'hello' to an old friend." Jaime says to Joey.

Jaime hurries down to the end of the bar, spilling most of the contents of his drinks along the way.

"Greta!, I mean Sophie! What…..I mean how did you get here?!!!!!" Jaime stammers with an uncontained mixture of joy and disbelief.

"Well, after my lovely interment at the London Cage,

the Brits allowed me to continue my spying. You know, for the good of the cause! One night at 'The Hope' a very handsome American pilot walked in. He happened to be a very talented saxophone player as well. He played a spontaneous set at 'The Hope'. Then he swept me off my feet and off the isle of Great Britain. We live in Manhattan. He is playing here tonight with The Tommy Dorsey Band."

"Do you believe in love at first sight Mr. Winter?" she asks.

"Yes I do." Jaime replies as he glances into the crowd to find Gia sitting beside Gabrielle. He catches her eye and Gia returns his gaze with one of her brilliant and irresistible smiles. "Yes I certainly do!" he adds.

Jaime and Sophie raise their glasses. "To Greta and Gustav" Sophie says as they clink their glasses together. "To Greta and Gustav". Jaime repeats "Who were both on the right side of history." He leans in and kisses her cheek.

"Welcome to America! I think you'll like it here!" Jaime says.

"I think you are right! See you around, my favorite spy!" Sophie says with a mischievous smile on her face. She winks at Jaime and turns and walks away, disappearing as the crowd closes behind her. She makes her way to the backstage door.

'What a world! What a wonderful and crazy world!' Jaime thinks as he makes his way back to his table.

XLIV.   Yesterday

Gia and her son Anthony drive slowly through the town of Scituate. Gia takes in the surroundings. Surprisingly, the town has not changed much in fifty years. The quant village of North Scituate has remained the same. This is due to the fact that the reservoir providing the water supply to most of the state of Rhode Island is located in Scituate. It has kept the town unspoiled, preventing strip malls and super stores from building in the town.

The restricted woods that surround the reservoir are dotted with the ruins of the homes and structures of long-gone villages. The occupants of these long-forgotten settlements were forced to abandon their homes, businesses, schools, and farms to accommodate the development of the reservoir in the 1920's.

Gia wonders how time has gotten away from her, slipping by as if in fast motion. 'How is it that I have not returned to this beautiful town since I worked here fifty years ago' she thinks. Then she ponders, perhaps she wanted to keep the memory of it pristine. It is hallowed ground for her. After all, it is where she fell in love.

They pass over the horseshoe dam and past The Rhode Island State police barracks. They are headed to Chopmist

Hill, to visit what remains of the monitoring station Gia worked at during WWII.

It is December and the town is blanketed with freshly fallen snow. The snow sparkles, encouraged by the bright sunshine. Gia recalls that Scituate always got a considerable amount of snow compared to the rest of the state. She smiles, remembering the snowstorms that would keep everyone at the monitoring station stranded for days. They would play cards; drink brandy a bit too early in the day. Sometimes they would bundle up and take long walks through the woods. If they were lucky they would spot a deer, silently walking through the snow. A nearby brook, the only sound to disturb the tranquility of the moment.

They make the final turn onto the road where the monitoring station once existed. The dirt road Gia remembers has long since been paved. The rolling fields of farmland have been replaced with oversized homes. Manicured gardens and backyard swimming pools have replaced the natural woodlands that Gia recalls.

As they round the last corner, Gia takes in a sharp breath. It is still there; she marvels at this fact. The old Victorian farmhouse still stands.

To the left of the house, the radio tower is still reaching for the sky. It is so out of place in this rural setting. It is rusted and covered in ivy now. But it still stand as if to say 'remember me? Nothing would have been possible without me'. It defiantly refuses to crumble, this monumental steel ghost of the past.

"Stop the car." Gia says as she stares at the house, the

grounds surrounding it. "Stop here." She adds. Anthony pulls the car to the side of the road. They sit in silence. Gia slowly opens her door and gets out. Anthony follows.

"Let's walk the rest of the way." She says to Anthony, wanting to take in the scenery from afar at first.

They both walk slowly up to the property; Gia is lost in her thoughts of the past.

"That's the porch, Anthony. That's where your father proposed to me." Gia says, her eyes welling with tears remembering that moment. It is all so brief, she thinks. Much too brief......Jaime is already gone, passing away before his time. Wasn't it yesterday we sat on that porch, sipping gin on a cold winter night. We were wrapped in a blanket together, laughing as we planned our future. She recalls the last thing Jaime said to her before he died. "I'll always be right beside you Gia.....wherever you go." And then he was gone.

They forego walking onto the property, not wanting to disturb the current owner. Instead, they walk along the road. They pass the stonewall, original to the property.

"There, those ruins over there." Gia points. "It's the old Quonset huts. It's where all the men stayed throughout the war. The women stayed in the house on the second floor." she explains to Anthony.

Most of the outbuildings still remain visible, although now they are crumbling ruins covered in snow. But they are there still, struggling to remain. Gia marvels at how the earth is taking back its land, slowly contributing to the decay of wood and steel built during wartime. It is taking its time, but the deed will be done at some point.

In time all traces of the Chopmist Hill monitoring station will disappear forever. Perhaps the radio tower will be the only structure to elude the natural decomposition that is taking place here, obstinate in its struggle to remain intact. It is as if it still has a story to tell. A long-forgotten story.

"Maybe we should knock on the door. Ask if we can walk the property. Take a closer look." Anthony suggests.

"I'd rather not. I have seen what I came to see. I'd like to leave the rest of my memories undisturbed. I'm enjoying the solitude of my own recollections, memories of meeting your father and growing to love him right here at this very place. I am content to remember the good that we did here and the joy that we felt when the war was finally over," Gia says, her voice trailing off. She is lost in her thoughts of the past.

As they walk towards to the car, Gia turns to look back at the farmhouse. Is that Jaime she sees, sitting there on the porch steps, motioning for her to come back? Willing her to come join him and sit next to him for a while as they did so long ago.

"Soon, Jaime," Gia whispers to herself. "I'll see you soon."

The End

Author's Note

I was inspired to write this story after reading an article in the Providence Journal. The article was written in 2015 by Tom Mooney called 'Global Eavesdroppers: In World War II, dozens of radio operators in Scituate dialed in to enemy conversations worldwide.' It tells of the little-known story of the Chopmist Hill listening post.

Radio transmissions were, in fact, intercepted by the employees of RID (Radio Intelligence Division of the Federal Communications Commission). The Chopmist Hill spy monitoring post significantly contributed to a victorious outcome for the Allied forces. The remains of the radio tower still exist today.

The various places Gia and Jaime visit throughout Rhode Island on their dates all existed in the 1940's. With the exception of Crescent Park, all still exist today.

The Looff Carousel in Riverside, Rhode Island was built in 1895 by Charles Looff. Saved and restored in the 1970's, it was placed on the National Register of Historic Sites and Places in 1976.

The Café Society nightclub in Greenwich Village, New York opened in 1938. It was the first integrated nightclub in the United States. Billie Holiday sang 'Strange Fruit' written by Abel Meeropol for the very first time at Café Society in 1939. The nightclub closed its doors in 1948.

Anne Morgan, daughter of J.P. Morgan, is known for her philanthropy. She actively aided the French in both WWI and WWII. She rented fourteen rooms at Le Bristol in 1940, sheltering and aiding in the escape of Jewish people fleeing Nazi occupied Paris. She did this seamlessly until the United States entered the war in December of 1941. This account was found in a book entitled *Le Bristol Paris* by Pierre Jammet.